ACKNOWLEDGMENTS

First, I'd like to thank God for blessing me with the gift to write and allowing me to express myself through the written word. I'd like to thank my mother, Lisa Hipps, who has always pushed me toward greatness and helped me through my darkest days. I love you, Mom! My twin sister, Paris Green; my brothers, Rayshawn and Treymond Hipps. My best friends, Sade Glover and Miqual Sherrell, and my goddaughter, Legacy Williams. Next, I'd like to thank my writing mentor, Travis Hunter, who continues to guide me through this industry and for having my best interest since day one. Travis, you're an amazing man and positive leader in my life. I love you dearly! Thank you, Zane and Charmaine, for believing in a seventeen-year-old and giving me a chance to be a part of your publishing family. And a big shout-out to all of the Strebor Streetz family. True Glory, Shameek Speight, Nikki Ferrell, Nisha Lanae, CoCo Mixon, Theresa Calhoun, Rosalyn Reed, Nakia, Maxine King, Uolanda, and the rest of the family. My author friends; Sa'Id Salaam, Rasheed Carter, Patron Gold, Fire&Ice, Treasure Blue, Pinky Dior, and Jason Hooper. My cosmetology teacher from Oliver [illegible] School, Yevett Wells, who I love so much! [illegible] God for you. You're an amazing w[illegible] in the cosmetology field. My cosm[illegible] amye Williams, Camille Pinno, C[illegible] aitlyn

Rossa, and Jayme. My family, CEO Swift, Darius Jones, Wayne Simpson, Jenean Banks, Amanda Jones, Cheyanne Jones, Darius Jones Jr., Omminie McMahon, Sharon Pritchard, and Mikayla McMahon. My principal, Heath Bailey, Russian basketball player, J.R. Holden, Mr. Hacket, Mr. Hoffman, Mr. Spehar, and to all my loyal and amazing readers who've had my back through it all! Thank you!

Strebor on the Streetz

FAMILY OVER EVERYTHING

Strebor on the Streetz

Family Over Everything

PAIGE GREEN

SBI
Strebor Books
New York London Toronto Sydney

SBI
Strebor Books
P.O. Box 6505
Largo, MD 20792
http://www.streborbooks.com

ISBN 978-1-59309-501-7
ISBN 978-1-4767-1158-4 (ebook)
LCCN 2012951573

First Strebor Books trade paperback edition May 2013

Cover design: www.mariondesigns.com
Cover photograph: © Keith Saunders/Marion Designs

10 9 8 7 6 5 4 3 2 1

Manufactured in the United States of America

This novel is dedicated to all the young adults and teenagers who are lost and trying to find a way through this world. Every day is a struggle, yet with faith, belief, and guidance, anything is possible. Never allow anyone to define you or tell you that you can't reach your goals. You can do anything and everything you set your mind to do. The sky is the limit, reach for the stars!

This novel is also dedicated to Chaz "Big Chaz" Anger, may you rest in peace. We all love and miss you. This book is also dedicated to the loving memory of the beautiful Ladrea "Drea" Freeman. Drea, not a day goes by that we don't think about you. The wounds are still fresh and although it hurts, we know God has gained an angel. We love and miss you. Rest peacefully.

PROLOGUE

Deion Jenkins stepped out of his black-on-black BMW with his date, Yoka, by his side. Dressed in an all-black Italian suit with a gray vest and silver cufflinks adorning his wrists, he gazed at Yoka, biting down on his lip, admiring her chocolate complexion. Turning, the twenty-three-year-old smiled as Yoka held on to his arm tightly as they then made their way down the red carpet, and into the Soldiers and Sailors building.

"Congratulations on the book!"

"Go, Deion!"

"You did it, my brother!" he heard a few people cheer as he finally walked through the front doors. The Soldiers and Sailors building was crowded inside and out with Deion's friends and new supporters, who were there to help him celebrate his novel, *Hustling Hard*. It had released over four months ago and more than 6,000 copies had sold.

Deion nodded his head in response, silently thanking them all as he kept a Colgate smile on his face and waved to a few people. Making his way into the auditorium, which was filled to capacity with all of his supporters, he watched as Yoka took a seat in a reserved chair in the front. He walked onto the stage, grabbed a microphone, and cleared his throat.

The audience immediately became quiet as they gave Deion their undivided attention.

"I want to thank you all for your love, support, and for believing in me. I started writing this novel at sixteen and finally got it published a couple of months ago. While writing *Hustling Hard*, I was going through a rough time in my life," he said before briefly pausing. "But with the help of my former literature teacher, Ms. Younger, I was able to overcome that difficult time and write my novel. Even though she couldn't make it today, I'm still thankful for her."

"I know that's right!" someone from the audience yelled.

"I'd also love to thank my late mother, Melissa Johnson, who left this earth eight years ago. My mother believed in me and I know that if she was here today, she'd be in tears. Thank you all again, and I hope you enjoy reading this novel as much as I enjoyed writing it."

Almost everyone in the auditorium stood to their feet as they clapped and cheered for Deion. Flashing a bright smile, he held onto the microphone and then walked off the stage and made his way toward a nearby table, where he'd be autographing his paperback and hardcover books.

Taking a seat at the table, he placed the microphone on it, and then folded his hands. He watched as a man dressed in an expensive gray Gucci suit walked up to his table. "Congratulations, my brother! Look at you; you finally made it!"

Staring at the man, Deion quickly stood back to his feet and walked up to the man. "Jarell? Whoa, my man! How long has it been?"

"It's been eight years, Deion!" Jarell, Deion's childhood friend, replied. "I see you finally made it and you're doing your thing! I'm so proud of you, my brother!"

"Thank you, Jarell. I appreciate it. What's been up with you, though? That suit is fresh!" Deion said with admiration.

"I've been working, you know? I own a barbershop and have three kids now."

"Oh, really? You're not hustling anymore? That's what's up!"

"Yeah, of course I'm hustling; just not the illegal way. There's money in the barbershop industry. I had to change my life for my kids, you know?" Jarell replied and then raised his eyebrows. "Where's your brother and sister at? I haven't seen them in years either. Are they here?"

"Look, I have to finish signing these books, so I'm going to catch you later," Deion said, dismissing Jarell's question.

Nodding his head with confusion, Jarell watched as Deion walked back to his table, took a seat, and grabbed a marker to finish autographing copies of his readers' books.

For the next hour, Deion laughed and mingled with his newfound family, his supporters.

"What's up, man? How are you?" Deion asked a dark-skinned man as he opened up his paperback copy of *Hustling Hard* before passing it to Deion.

"I'm good; congratulations on your book. I want to thank you for writing about the struggle and letting these people know how hard it is to live and raise our children in the projects."

"You're welcome; thank you for your support."

The man nodded his head before walking away. As the night progressed and the party started to come to an end, Deion rose to his feet, grabbed the microphone from the signing table, and started to thank everyone for coming. He watched as a familiar face made his way toward him, causing his breath to catch in his throat.

It was Day'onne.

"What's up, Deion? Why it look like you seen a ghost?" Day'onne said, smiling mischievously as he walked up to Deion.

Day'onne, who was dressed in a black-and-white Puma jogging suit and all-black Puma sneakers, folded his masculine hands together as he stood in front of Deion.

Placing the microphone back on the table, Deion gritted his teeth as his eyes narrowed into angry slits. "What the hell are you doing here? You weren't invited!"

"Damn, why all that? I can't stop to congratulate my own twin for his accomplishments?"

"Alright, you said it. Now bounce, man," Deion replied as he started to walk away.

Grabbing him by his wrist, Day'onne glared at his brother. "Oh, so now that you got a little bit of success, you want to act shady? I haven't seen you in over eight years and this is all I get?"

"What do you want from me, Day'onne?" Deion growled as he snatched his arm away from him.

Clenching his jaw, Day'onne simply replied, "I want you to come and work with me."

Looking at Day'onne, Deion threw his head back in laughter. "Risk my life to be a drug dealer? You must be crazy! I already can't stand being around you, so please tell me why I should come and work for you?"

"What? You out here writing books about hustling when you don't have a clue about it!" Day'onne shouted, causing a handful of people to turn toward them.

"Look, I have my own thing going on with this writing, Day'onne. I don't need nor want your drug money," he replied in almost a whisper.

"This ain't about money, Deion!"

"What's it about, then?" Deion asked with confusion.

Biting down on his lip as he gazed Deion directly into his eyes, Day'onne asked, "Do you remember Jewels from Northview?"

"Jewels? Yeah, I remember him. Why?"

"Well, he got out of jail a couple of months ago and, from what I'm hearing, he's looking for all three of us."

Confused, Deion frowned. "Why would he be looking for us?"

"This ain't the place to discuss it, Deion. Jarell gave me your number a little earlier. I'll be calling you in a few days. When I do, answer the phone," Day'onne ordered and then turned and walked away.

CHAPTER ONE
THE BEGINNING...

Twenty-four-year-old Relisha Jenkins lay sprawled out in the middle of her living room, gripped with fatigue and paralyzed with pain. Her boyfriend of two years, Derrick, sat on a nearby sofa, sniffing lines of cocaine and drinking shots of tequila. Briefly tossing his head back as the deadly drug raced through his system, Derrick threw his head forward before flaring his nose and standing to his feet. With a crazed look in his eyes, he balled his hands into tight fists as he stared down at Relisha. "Didn't I tell you I wanted you in the house an hour ago? Where the hell were you?"

"Nothing, baby!" Relisha cried, her voice trembling in fear. "I told you I was out shopping with Gina!"

Not believing her, Derrick flared his nose up as he bent down onto his knees, grabbed a handful of her hair, and began to drag her out of the living room and into their bedroom.

"Please stop!" she cried as she tried to grab a hold of his wrists, but it was to no avail.

When Derrick finally reached their bedroom door, he continued to drag her until they were completely in the bedroom before he released the strong hold he had on her hair, causing her head to smack against the hard floor. Reaching down, he wrapped his arms around her neck before lifting her off of the floor, placed her against their dresser and slammed her against the mirror.

Relisha winced and cried in pain as the mirror shattered, causing tiny shards of glass to pierce her skin.

"Your ass better start listening to me, do you hear me?" Derrick yelled as he shook her violently by her neck.

With her eyes rolling to the back of her head, she struggled to nod her head as Derrick unwrapped his ashy hands from around her neck, causing her to gasp for air. Derrick continued to smack her around until he had no energy left in him.

"Get the hell up and go make my money since you want to be so damn sneaky," Derrick yelled as he kicked Relisha, who was now lying almost motionless on the floor, before walking out of the room.

Moaning in pure agony, Relisha cried from the pain that taunted at her as she sat up, grabbed the corner of her bed, and used it as a crutch to stand to her feet. Her knees buckled, yet she kept her composure as she slowly limped out of the room and into the bathroom before closing the door behind herself. Glancing at herself in the mirror, she quickly gazed away, ashamed of the sight of her busted lip and swollen eye. Grabbing a washcloth from the top of her toilet, she turned the sink on, dampened her cloth, and began to wipe the blood and tears off of her face. When she was done, she tossed the washcloth onto the back of the toilet before opening up the bathroom door and making her way out. Walking back into her bedroom, she made her way toward her closet before bending down to retrieve her duffle bag. Briefly closing her eyes as she bit down on her lip, she grabbed the small of her back, her knees trembling, as she grabbed a hold of her bag, and sighed as she stood back to her feet. Gently tossing the duffle bag over her shoulder, she slowly walked toward the front door and left to go to work.

✠ ✠ ✠

An hour later, Relisha limped into Club 412. With her hair tied into a sloppy bun, a pair of shapeless, baggy sweat pants nearly hanging off of her plump behind, and a tattered shirt hanging off of her shoulders, she ignored the numerous glares as she headed toward the dressing room.

"Damn, what the hell happened to her? Derrick must still be whooping her ass," a stripper named Delicious said as Relisha finally entered the room.

Disregarding Delicious, Relisha walked past her before she undressed out of her clothes and tossed them to the side. Opening her bag, she pulled out a gold bikini set, changed into it and gazed at herself in the full-length mirror on the wall. Admiring her stallion-like legs, thin waist, and caramel complexion, Relisha glanced at herself before she bent back down, reached into her duffle bag, and pulled out her small makeup kit. Applying a huge amount of foundation on her face, along with mascara and gold eye shadow that complemented her slanted eyes, she pulled out a spray bottle, sprayed the water throughout her hair, and ran her fingers through her roots as she watched her hair turn into long, ringlet curls. Glancing into the mirror, she noticed Delicious and a few irrelevant strippers enviously gazing at her curvy physique. She took a deep breath, turned back around, and finally made her way back out of the dressing room and toward the stage.

Walking onto the stage, she nodded toward the disc jockey before gripping the thick gold pole, arched her back, and patiently waited for the music to start. Skimming the crowd, she saw that the club was filled to capacity, almost like every weekend, with people who wanted to witness the infamous Relisha work her magic tricks on the pole.

When Nelly's "Tip Drill," blared through the speakers, Relisha skidded her hands toward the floor. With her face down and ass up, she hopped to the balls of her feet before she started to gyrate to the music. Moving flawlessly like the professional she was, the crowd exploded and threw a large amount of bills onto the stage.

After dancing for two more songs, she bent down, gathered her money, and ran off of the stage and back into the dressing room. Stepping back into her shirt and sweat pants, she tossed the bag back over her shoulders before discreetly hightailing it out of the club.

✠ ✠ ✠

"How much did you make tonight?" Derrick asked as Relisha walked into the front door.

"Two thousand," she replied as she fidgeted with her fingers and eyed the floor like a child.

Derrick, who was seated on the couch, got to his feet and walked over to Relisha. Snatching the duffle bag off her shoulder, he reached into it and pulled the money out of it. He stuffed it into his pockets, tossed the duffle bag into her face, and walked away.

Bending down and picking up the bag after it had fallen, she peered into it and shook her head when there wasn't at least one bill left in it.

For the first year of Relisha and Derrick's relationship, Derrick cherished her and nearly kissed the ground that she walked on. He catered to her every need, uplifted her during the difficult times, and laughed with her during the good times. Although he was a notorious drug lord at the time, Relisha looked past that and loved him for him. But after the first year, things started to

go down the drain. The good times became a distant memory and the bad times became their new reality. After becoming addicted to his own drug product, Derrick slowly but surely lost his power and respect as one of the biggest leaders of Pittsburgh's drug cartels. Once he was a full-blown addict and lost everything, he lashed out all of his anger and frustration on Relisha. He abused her mentally, physically, sexually, and emotionally. But being deeply in love with him, she stayed, silently hoping she'd have her old Derrick back. But as she stood there, in the middle of her living room, holding an empty duffle with a bruised heart, Relisha finally came to the conclusion that enough was enough. She threw the bag back on the floor before she stormed off toward him.

"I'm so tired of this! You think you can keep taking my money that I bust my ass for, so you can smoke it up? I think not!" she yelled as she balled her fingers into tight fists and narrowed her eyes.

"What? Who you think you talking to?" he yelled as he turned around to face her.

Relisha, whose chest was heaving, started to walk up closer toward him before he gritted his teeth, ran toward her, and lunged at her. Grabbing her by her neck, he then lifted her into the air before he slammed her onto the floor, instantly causing her to arch her back in pain.

"You crazy? How dare you try to put your hands on me, woman? I'll kill your ass!" he yelled as he started to kick her.

Curling into a ball, her body violently shook as he continued to pound her body with his feet. Once he briefly stopped to catch his breath, Relisha took it as her only chance. She mustered up all of the strength that she had from within, uncurled herself from her ball, and lifted her feet into the air, delivering a hard kick to Derrick's testicles.

Gasping, Derrick doubled over as he clutched his testicles and his eyes nearly rolled to the back of his head as he fell to the floor and groaned. Relisha weakly forced herself to her knees and slowly crawled on all fours, as if she was a dog. Making her way toward the kitchen, her body throbbed with every move. When she finally made it into the kitchen, she crawled toward the cabinet under the sink, opened it, and pulled out Derrick's .357 handgun.

"What you gon' do with that?" Derrick growled as he held on to the kitchen wall with one hand and his crotch with the other hand.

Ignoring him as she got up, Relisha gripped the gun in her hand and aimed it at him.

"Get that shit out of my face! Are you crazy?"

Twisting up her nose as she stared at Derrick through her scornful eyes and shaking her head in disbelief. she finally took heed to how the love of her life had drastically changed for the worst. Derrick's masculine features, soft, creamy brown skin, and long dreadlocks were long gone. Now, he was a shell of his old image, nearly a hundred pounds with matted dreads and an empty look in his eyes.

Cocking the gun as she placed her hand on the trigger, she said, "I will no longer be your punching bag, Derrick. Goodbye, my love." She squeezed the trigger three times and watched as all three bullets pierced his chest, instantly killing him.

Jadedly making her way out of the kitchen, she stared at his lifeless body one last time before making her way toward her bedroom. Walking into it and reaching into her closet, she pulled out all of her clothes and the rest of her belongings before she packed them up and left their apartment for good.

✠✠✠

A couple of months after Relisha killed Derrick, she became homeless. She went from living on the streets and eating out of garbage cans to living in homeless shelters. After losing a large amount of weight from lack of eating daily, Relisha lost her job at Club 412 and just when she thought that things couldn't get any worse, she found out she was pregnant with twins. Completely broken and having nowhere to turn, she finally made it back to the neighborhood where she was born and raised, Northview Heights.

Even though Northview Heights was a high-crime neighborhood, it was still home for her. When she arrived back, five months' pregnant with twin boys, and appearing shattered, she stopped at her old neighbor, Melissa Johnson's, house and knocked on the door.

When Melissa answered the door and noticed Relisha, she welcomed her in with warming arms. Melissa, who was in her mid-thirties, was a kindhearted woman who went out of her way to help and provide for a pregnant Relisha. She showered her with motherly love, gave her food, clothes, and a place to rest her head. But after Relisha gave birth to her twin sons, naming them Deion and Day'onne, she started to take advantage of Melissa. She would stay out late hours of the night while Melissa stayed up in the house taking care of the twins. At first, Melissa didn't speak too much on it, reasoning she was acting out on all of the things that she'd been through. But when the twins turned one and Relisha failed to show up on their birthday, she'd had enough.

"Hey, girl!" Relisha said as she staggered into Melissa's apartment.

It was one in the morning and as Melissa sat there in the living room, with her legs and hands crossed, she shook her head in pity as the strong smell of marijuana and alcohol assaulted her nose.

"Look, baby girl, you have to go. Not now, but right now," Melissa said as she stood up.

"What the hell you mean I got to go? This is my house, too!" Relisha yelled, her words slurring.

"I'm sorry, but last time I checked, I pay the bills in here while you rip and run the streets. You have two boys to take care of but you'd rather party and stay out? I've had enough of it! Your clothes are already packed at the door."

"Yeah, whatever! You can keep those bastard kids here! I couldn't care less about all of you!" she yelled as she stormed toward the door, grabbed her clothes, and wobbled out of the front door.

An hour later, Relisha showed up at Club 412 in a baggy sweat suit that hung off of her rail-thin frame. Judging by her sunken eyes, thin hair, and rail-thin frame, most of the people she bypassed had mistaken her as a drug addict. Her once flawless physique and erotic features had vanished long ago. That day was the first time she'd been at the club in months. As she started to make her way toward the dressing room, almost everyone she passed dropped their mouths in shock.

"What the hell happened to you?" Delicious chuckled, folding her arms under her breasts as Relisha walked into the dressing room.

Relisha rolled her eyes to the back of her head as she began to strip out of the sweat suit and changed into a baby blue bikini that hung off of her body.

"I know you aren't going out there like that?" another stripper asked with a frown.

Relisha continued to ignore them as she strutted out the dressing room and walked onto the stage.

The disc jockey hesitated to play the music at first, but after noticing the murderous glare on her face, he gave in. When Plies'

song "Plenty Money" roared throughout the club, Relisha bit down on her lip as she arched her small back and gripped the pole. The crowd erupted into loud, thunderous laughter as they watch her try too hard to make her small booty meat shake. Relisha tried her best to ignore the laughter, but after she didn't notice not one dollar thrown on the stage, she instantly knew she was making a fool of herself.

Gripped with embarrassment, Relisha ran off the stage with tears blurring her vision. After arriving back into the dressing room, she collapsed on the chair and cried her heart out.

"Damn, girl, you look bad," Delicious said, taking a blunt out of her bra before taking a long pull at it.

Relisha looked at her nemesis, teary-eyed and full of sorrow. She knew she had made a complete fool out of herself and it was tearing her up inside as she noticed the sly smile on Delicious' face.

"Let me hit that blunt!" Relisha said, ignoring her smart remark.

"You sure? It's..."

"It's what? Pass the blunt," she yelled before snatching the blunt out of Delicious' hand and taking a long pull.

Delicious smiled mischievously as she watched Relisha take a few puffs from the blunt before she awkwardly looked at it. "It's laced, you dumb bitch!" Delicious laughed.

CHAPTER TWO

As time progressed and months turned into years, Relisha transformed into a full-blown drug addict. Since the day that she had smoked her nemesis' laced marijuana, she went from smoking them three times a week to sniffing pure cocaine daily. She watched as her body went from petite to emaciate in a matter of months after she'd gotten addicted to the drug. Relisha was on a path of destruction and with her twin sons seldom on her mind, another challenging situation seemed to draw her thoughts on her boys back.

One day, Relisha walked through the cold streets of Northview with a vial of cocaine in her hand. Wearing disheveled clothing, she stared around the dull neighborhood through her bloodshot eyes, searching for a place to take her drugs. When she finally found a place in a dark alley, she threw herself against a dirty wall and slowly slid down it. Reaching into her pocket and pulling out a small mirror and a rolled-up dollar bill, she took the vial of cocaine, poured it on the mirror and proceeded to divide it into three lines until she felt a sharp pain shoot through her stomach, causing her to drop the mirror and double over.

"Ugh!" she screamed as she felt an extreme amount of pressure coming from her lower abdomen.

With her chest heaving, she spread her legs and arched her back when her uterus contracted and she felt something ripping through her vaginal canal.

Shifting her body from off of the wall, she then placed her elbows on the ground as she lay on her back and took slow, deep breaths. Closing her eyes tightly, she released a loud scream as her body started to shake uncontrollably and she then felt a strong urge to push.

Sitting up, she kicked her sweat pants off as she continued to push and scream. Reaching in between her legs, and touching her vagina, her heart almost leapt out of her throat when she felt the head of her unborn child crowning. She clenched her teeth and tossed her head back as she continued to push. Five minutes later, she reached back down, grabbed the baby by its shoulders, and pulled the rest of its body out of her before she cradled it in her arms.

The baby lay almost motionless in her arms as Relisha then took her small mirror, smacked it against the ground, took a broken piece, and cut the umbilical cord. Picking up her sweat pants, she wrapped them around the baby before mustering up what strength she had within, and rose to her feet. Panicking, she ran out of the alleyway with the baby in her arms and aimlessly walked through Northview. When she saw a garbage can in the distance, she started to walk toward it until she thought about her twins. She turned and walked in the opposite direction. When she made it to Melissa's porch, she placed the baby on the ground, banged on the door, and then ran off the porch, disappearing into the dark night.

✠✠✠

Melissa sat at her kitchen table, tears seeping from her eyes. With her hair pulled back in a tight bun and dressed in a knee-length skirt with a white shirt, she turned her face away from

eight-year-old Deion, who ran around the kitchen with his toy truck in his hand.

Peering at the stack of bills on her table, she dropped her head into her hands as Deion walked up to her and asked, "Are you okay, Mom?"

Melissa looked at Deion, trying her best to mask her pain as she flashed a fake smile and nodded her head. "Yes, baby, I'm okay… why do you ask?"

"I thought you were crying."

"I'm fine, baby. Go ahead and play with…"

A loud knocking coming from her front door interrupted her. She hopped out of her chair and walked toward it. Looking out the peephole, she didn't see anyone there, and she shook her head and opened the door. "I'm so tired of these kids playing on my darn door!"

When she gazed around outside and still didn't see anyone, she started to close the door until she caught a glimpse of what lay on her threshold. Bending down as tears formed into her eyes, the sight of a thin, pale baby wrapped in wet rags burned a hole through her heart. She lifted it into her arms and stepped back inside before she closed the door behind her.

The infant's skin was cold and pasty as Melissa unwrapped the dirty sweat pants from its body.

"Whose baby is that?" Day'onne asked, hopping off the floral sofa.

"I don't know, Day'onne. Deion, please go get my purse and keys from off my bed. Hurry up!" she yelled.

Judging by the umbilical cord that still hung from the infant's body, she knew it was birthed into this world not too long ago.

"Here you go, Mom!" Deion yelled as he handed Melissa her purse and keys.

"C'mon, y'all, put your shoes and coats on!"

The twins nodded their heads as they ran to the living room closet and stepped into their shoes and coats. When they were ready, they ran out of the front door with Melissa, who was still holding the motionless baby, following right after them. She strapped the twins in her car before handing the baby to Deion. "Be careful, baby. Hold it until we get to the hospital."

Nodding his head, Deion stared at Day'onne, who was frowning at the baby, before he asked, "Do you think it's dead?"

"I don't know, and I damn sure don't care," Day'onne replied before he turned toward the window and stared out it.

"Don't worry, baby, we'll save you," Deion whispered to the infant as Melissa placed her key in the ignition before driving off.

When they finally arrived at Allegheny General Hospital, Melissa quickly hopped out the driver's seat before running to the backseat, opening the door, and gently taking the baby out of Deion's arms. With the twins following behind her, she ran to the emergency department, and yelled, "Help me, please!"

A handful of doctors ran to her, noticing the pale, almost lifeless infant dangling in her arms. One of the doctors gently took the newborn and placed it on a gurney.

"What happened here, ma'am?" one of the doctors asked as they rushed the baby toward the NICU department.

"I don't know; I found her in front of my house. Someone placed her there," Melissa replied as she ran with the doctors, refusing to leave the baby's side.

"We're going to need you to stay out here while we do our jobs," another doctor said when they finally reached NICU.

Nodding her head, she stopped in her tracks as she watched the doctors disappear into the distance.

For the next three days, Melissa had been at the hospital con-

sistently to answer questions from the police, who were trying to find the mother and to get an update on the infant who had stolen her heart. The doctors hadn't been any help, only alerting Melissa that the baby was doing much better than before. But on the fourth day, Melissa and the twins walked into the waiting room and she started to demand more details.

A doctor walked right up to her. "Are you Melissa Johnson?"

"Yes, I am."

"Okay, my name is Dr. Harrison and I'm sorry we haven't given you a lot of details on the baby. We aren't used to someone dropping off a baby they found and then sticking around."

"It's fine. Please tell me what's going on with the baby?"

She watched nervously as Dr. Harrison removed his bifocal glasses from his face and placed them into his lab coat. Taking a deep breath, he stared into Melissa's eyes. "It's a girl. This child has been born addicted to crack cocaine, Ms. Johnson. Her health was steadily decreasing and she had a low birth weight. We ran tests to make sure she wasn't born with any mental problems, too."

"Was she?"

"No, she wasn't born with any mental problems. That child is a fighter, Ms. Johnson. Her health is increasing and she's doing much better."

"Can we see her, Mom?" Deion intervened with a bright smile on his face.

Gazing at the doctor with pleading eyes, Melissa smiled when Dr. Harrison smiled back at Deion and nodded his head. He started to lead them toward the NICU until Melissa noticed Day'onne still standing in the waiting room.

"Are you coming, son?" she asked as she walked back toward him.

"No, I'm not going. I don't want to see that baby," he replied with knitted eyebrows and a twisted mouth.

"Why not, baby?"

"I'm just tired, Mom. I'll wait for y'all in here," he lied as he took a seat.

Eyeing him one last time, she nodded her head before she turned around and walked quickly, catching up with Deion and Dr. Harrison.

Once they reached the unit where the baby was located, Dr. Harrison opened the door to a small room and led them inside. "You two have five minutes."

They nodded their heads when they watched him walk out of the room. Walking up to the baby's incubator, Melissa and Deion smiled as they peered down at her.

"Wow, she's beautiful, Mommy."

"Yes she is, son. She's almost the same color as you were when you were first born."

The baby's skin color was now a light brown, no longer pale. She had jet-black, wavy hair and a pin-straight nose.

When the baby opened her eyes, Melissa couldn't help but think of how familiar her light, slanted eyes look. Gasping, realization hit her and everything started to make sense. The baby being born addicted to cocaine, and her light eyes led to one conclusion. She glanced at Deion's slanted eyes before she stared into the baby's eyes.

"What's wrong, Mom?"

"Deion, baby. This is your sister."

"How? You didn't have her?" he asked confusedly.

"No, baby. Remember your other mommy I told you and Day'onne about?" Eyeing the floor as he nodded his head. "That's her daughter, baby. Y'all have a sister!"

✠ ✠ ✠

For the next couple of months, Melissa busied herself with work, looking after the twins, and making daily visits to the hospital.

Over time, the drug-addicted infant's health drastically improved, and one day when Melissa came to the hospital for her regular daily visit, she found a surprise.

"Hello, Ms. Johnson, My name is Diane Puchiarelli, and I'm from Child Protective Services."

"Hey, Ms. Puchiarelli, how may I help you?" Melissa asked skeptically, shaking the woman's hand.

"I've been assigned to this case. The infant in question was born addicted to crack cocaine and abandoned. I've been told that you've been a consistent visitor?"

"Yes, but what are you getting at, Ms. Puchiarelli?" she asked.

"Well, I have been informed that this child's health is improving and she's healthy enough to be discharged. They're ready for her to be released and since we don't know who her biological parents are, it's my job to get her into a foster home or assign her a legal guardian, immediately."

"Okay, is that where I come in?"

Ms. Puchiarelli shook her head as she folded her arms under her breasts. "I'm not certain. I did a brief background check on you and discovered you live in the high-crime area, Northview Heights. This child has already been through a lot, and it's my job to make sure she's properly taken care of and in a safe environment."

"Are you saying because I live there, it isn't safe for her?"

"Yes, but—"

"Excuse me, but for your information, I took in two twin boys over seven years ago whose mother, like that child in there, abandoned them. Because I live in Northview doesn't mean she'd be in danger. There's danger everywhere in this city, not to men-

tion this world! That child in that nursery waiting to be released is mine!"

Ms. Puchiarelli nodded her head as she remained silent for a moment, trying to choose her words more carefully before she spoke. Having dealt with numerous cases where children were placed with money-hungry, careless guardians who only wanted them for the paychecks the government provided for them, she could tell Melissa was different.

"I can see that you care for this child. Perhaps I should reconsider my position. I don't want her to go through any more than she's already been through."

"I can understand that, but I'd never hurt her. Why do you think I pop my head up here every day? Just like you, I want the best for her, too," Melissa assured her.

Ms. Puchiarelli smiled. "I know that now. Give me some time and I'll have the paperwork ready. You're on your way to becoming her legal guardian."

For the next couple of days, Melissa took her time signing papers. On the day the baby was scheduled to be released, she arrived at the hospital with a huge smile on her face and carrying a new outfit she'd bought for the little girl to wear home.

"Congratulations, Ms. Johnson; take care of this beautiful child," Dr. Harrison said as Melissa dressed her.

"What are you going to name her?" Mrs. Puchiarelli asked.

"Corrine. Corrine Johnson."

That night, when Melissa arrived home, she took the baby upstairs to her bedroom. When she'd found out that Corrine would be a member of her family, she'd quickly gotten rid of her king-sized bed for a twin size, so that she'd be able to fit a baby crib in her room.

"Whose baby is that?" Day'onne asked in a low, icy tone, startling Melissa.

"Boy, what are you doing up?"

"I heard you come in. I asked, whose baby is that?"

"Mine. She's your new baby sister. Her name is Corrine," Melissa said, flashing a bright smile before placing her into the crib.

"Sister? That bitch ain't my sister!" Day'onne spat harshly.

Without warning, Melissa charged off of her bed, grabbed him by his arm, and slapped him continuously on his behind with her hands. Day'onne laughed hysterically with every hit she delivered to him. When she noticed the whupping wasn't doing anything to him, as always, she stopped hitting him.

"Look at me, Day'onne!"

He flared his nose and clenched his jaw as she forcefully grabbed him by his chin, forcing him to meet her eyes.

"If I ever hear you call your sister or any female another name, that's your behind!" she stated firmly. "Understand?"

He nodded as he turned to leave. Before he walked out of the room, he cut his eyes at Melissa. "Melissa, I will never respect a female. My own damn momma didn't respect me, so why should I respect them?"

Melissa was at a loss for words as she watched him walk away. Something in the pit of her soul told her Day'onne would forever mean what he said.

CHAPTER THREE

Seven-year-old Corrine lay in her bed, tightly wrapped up in her sheets. Her body jittered when she felt a cold pair of hands tugging at her covers and legs.

"Please don't do this!" she cried as she tried her best to pull away from him.

Fifteen-year-old Day'onne ignored her as he grabbed the sheets with both hands and pulled them completely off of her body.

Shuddering, Corrine closed her eyes as he grabbed a hold of her wrists, pinned them behind her head, and pulled her pajama pants down. Parting her legs with his, he pulled down his shorts and vigorously entered her.

Arching her back, she wailed out a loud, heart-wrenching scream, causing him to quickly place his hands over her mouth. With tears blurring her vision, her body shook with agony as Day'onne continued to pound her youthful body, shattering her young soul and stripping her from her innocence.

After five minutes passed, and Day'onne still was torturing her with each stroke, Corrine finally stopped fighting back. Her body went limp.

He wickedly laughed. "Good girl, there you go. Take it."

Two minutes later, he pulled his penis out of her and ejaculated on her stomach. She cringed as she watched him climb off of her, pick the sheet off the floor, and begin to wipe his penis

off with it. He then pulled up his shorts and made his way toward her bedroom door before he turned around. "You better not tell Melissa."

✠ ✠ ✠

It was a bright summer morning in Northview Heights. The hustlers were out hugging the street corners, selling drugs in order to feed their families, while the young children ran around, cracking fire hydrants open and getting wet in the middle of the streets.

Day'onne stepped off of his front porch, taking in the atmosphere as he made his way through the neighborhood. Dressed in a pair of red basketball shorts, a red T-shirt, and a pair of all-white Air Force Ones, he looked like a normal, rough-looking teenage boy. His unbraided hair was pulled back into a loose ponytail and his eyes glistened in the sun.

As he made his way toward his best friend, Menace's house, with a scowl on his face, he watched as bystanders eyed the ground, refusing to glance in his direction. He ignored them all, chuckling as he finally made it to Menace's front porch. Menace, who was a black-blue, fifteen-year-old boy, sat on his porch with a glowering look on his face.

"What's up with you?" Day'onne asked, giving him a hand dap.

"Nothing; where's the weed at?"

"I don't know; I'm broke," Day'onne replied as he patted his hands against his shorts. "Do you have some money?"

Digging his hands into his pockets, Menace shook his head before he snapped his fingers. "Nope, but you already know what time it is, don't you?"

Nodding, Day'onne glanced across the street before he turned

to Menace. "Yeah, there go little Rich and Guns over there now. Let's go get them."

Standing to his feet, Menace followed after him, crossing the street and making their way toward Rich and Guns, two of many of Northview's drug dealers.

Rich and Guns, who were too busy serving a drug addict, didn't noticed Day'onne and Menace approaching them as they grabbed them from behind, wrapping their arms around their necks.

"Give it up," Day'onne said as he tightened the already stronghold he hand on Guns.

In a panic, Rich and Guns reached into their pockets and pulled out wads of cash and held them up to Day'onne and Menace as they gasped for air.

Grabbing the money out of their hands, Day'onne stuffed it into his pocket. He gripped Guns' neck even tighter and smiled as he watched a weak Guns squirm in his arms like a fish out of water. Clawing at Day'onne's arms, Guns' esophagus started to close in as he took slow, deep breaths and his vision became blurry.

Menace did the same to Rich as they watched both of them lose consciousness. They unwrapped their arms from around their necks, watched as they collapsed to the ground, and then walked away.

Crossing the street again, they walked into Menace's apartment and closed the door behind them. They took a seat and Day'onne pulled the money out of his pocket. Just as Day'onne proceeded to count, the stench emitting from Menace's living room and kitchen briefly broke his concentration.

Menace's living room was nearly empty and dirty, consisting of a couch and wooden table, and needed a good mopping. His kitchen only had a few pieces of silverware, a table, and a refrigerator that had rotten food spoiling in it.

Placing his hand over his nose, Day'onne said, "Damn, man. When you gonna get this place cleaned?"

"I don't know and honestly, I don't care. I'm trying to save up enough money, so I can get out of here," Menace replied.

Nodding, Day'onne turned his attention back to his money as he started to count it. When he was done, he stared at Menace. "Four hundred dollars? I'm tired of this, man. This is chump change. When are we gonna get some real money?"

"We can if we stop robbing for money and actually start making it."

"How, though?"

"Dealing. Stick-ups ain't gonna get us far. We need to start serving these fiends."

"But with four hundred dollars? That wouldn't even get us a brick of cocaine, yo. I don't know, man," Day'onne said, throwing his hands up in surrender.

"What we need to do is stop robbing these nickel-and-dime hustlers and start getting the ones with the real dough."

Rubbing the peach fuzz on his chin, Day'onne smiled and nodded his head. "You right. What about that dude, Crazy-Kay?"

Menace threw his head back in laughter before he stared at Deion. "Are you serious? He ain't making no money!"

"Well, you try, then!"

Menace balled his up his hand and tapped it against the other one before he snapped his finger a moment later, and said, "What about that dude, Jewels? How could we forget about him?"

A devious grin spread across Day'onne's face."Yeah, Menace! I have a plan!"

CHAPTER FOUR

Melissa was in her station wagon as she rode through Pittsburgh, fighting to keep her eyes open. That day, she had worked another twelve-hour shift at Pitt University as a security guard and as she tapped her fingers against the steering wheel, waiting for the light to change, she wondered about how much more her body could take.

Staring into the mirror, she glanced at the bags forming under her eyes before she turned her attention back to the road. When she finally made it up to Northview, she parked her car in front of her house and slowly stepped out of it.

"Hey, Ms. Melissa!"

"How are you, Ms. Melissa?"

"Hey, Momma Melissa!" a couple of people yelled at her as she made her way toward her home.

Flashing a smile, she waved at them and placed her key into the doorknob, unlocking the door, and walking in.

"Hey, Mom!" Corrine yelled as she ran up to Melissa and wrapped her arms around her waist.

"Hey, baby girl," Melissa said in a low tone as she took a seat on the couch.

Deion walked into the living room, took her purse out of her hands, and placed it on the living room table. Noticing Melissa's hunched shoulders, tensed arms, and weary eyes, Deion walked up

behind the couch and gently rubbed her shoulders. "Are you okay, Mom?"

"I'm fine, baby," she replied as Deion continued to massage her shoulders.

"Mom, did you get the food stamps, yet? Corrine and I are hungry. We've been eating bread and drinking water for the past week."

"They're coming soon, baby. I have some goodies in my purse for all of you."

Deion nodded his head and walked back in front of her, bent down for her purse, and handed it to her. He watched as she reached into it, pulled out a couple of bags of chips, and handed one to each of them.

Melissa fought back her tears as she watched them devour the chips like wild animals. Taking a deep breath, she dropped her head in silent prayer, asking God to give her strength. She got to her feet and walked toward her bedroom. Around that time, everything seemed to be falling apart for her. The government was threatening to cut off her food stamps, claiming she made too much money since she not only worked, but was receiving checks for adopting the twins and Corrine. She tried her best to keep food in all three of her children's mouths and clothes on their backs, but her eighty-year-old mother had recently been diagnosed with liver cancer and all of her money went to the nursing home and her medicine.

"Mommy, what's wrong?" Corrine asked, peeking through Melissa's bedroom door about an hour later.

Smiling, she nodded her head as she looked at the child she'd saved seven years prior. She loved the flourishing little girl. Taking a seat on the edge of her bed, Melissa waved for Corrine to enter. Corrine smiled as she ran into Melissa's arms.

Melissa then gazed down at her. "Corrine, you know you look exactly like your mother, right?"

"But, you're my mommy," she replied as she held her head down.

Placing her hand under her chin, Melissa lifted it up so that Corrine's eyes met hers. "I'm your mother, baby. But, I'm talking about your other mother. Do you remember her name?"

"Relaysha?"

Chuckling, Melissa said, "You're close, baby. Her name is Relisha. You know that she loves you as much as I do, right?"

"Why did she leave us then?"

"She wasn't in the right state of mind to take care of y'all, baby girl. But she does love all of you. You, Deion, and Day'onne," she said, briefly pausing. "Speaking of Day'onne, where is he?"

Melissa felt Corrine's arms tense up and caught a glimpse of fear in her eyes. "What's wrong, Corrine?"

"N-n-nothing, Momma," she replied and then gazed away.

"Are you lying to me, young lady?"

"No! I swear I'm not lying, Momma! I don't know where he is!" she yelled as tears cascaded down her cheeks.

"Okay, calm down, Corrine. Stop all of that crying." She watched as Corrine wiped the tears. "Now, go into the living room with Deion while I get some sleep, okay?"

"Okay; love you, Momma!"

"I love you, too, baby."

✠ ✠ ✠

It was one in the morning as Day'onne and Menace walked through Mt. Pleasant smoking marijuana and rapping Tupac lyrics. Both of them were dressed in their usual basketball shorts and

V-neck T-shirts. As they walked closer to their destination, Day'onne passed Menace the blunt as he continued to rap some of the lyrics from Tupac's "I Get Around."

"Finger tips on her hips, as I dip, gotta get a tight grip, don't slip, loose lips sinks ships. It's a trip. I love the way she lick her lips, see me jocking. Put a little twist in her hips, cause I'm watching!"

"I don't know why you singing that part, bro. You know damn well you don't get any," Menace joked.

"Yeah, okay. Yo momma ain't say that last night," he replied as Menace passed the blunt back to him.

"Chill out with all that."

"Don't get mad! But for real, is you ready to do this?" Day'onne asked before taking a long, deep pull of the blunt.

"Yeah, but you saying it like this the action; all we doing is buying guns!" Menace laughed as they walked up to a back door before knocking on it.

When the door finally opened, a big black man that went by the name Looney appeared in the doorway.

"What's up, little ones? What y'all here for?" Looney asked, scratching his potbelly.

Day'onne crunched his nose up in disgust. Looney, whose belly stuck out and hung low, was completely shirtless. His dark skin was decorated with even dark blotches. Day'onne almost vomited at the sight of him. "We here for some guns."

"Take a step into my office then, boys," Looney said as he moved out of the way and welcomed them into his basement. They were greeted by a fog of marijuana smoke, causing both of them to gasp for air. In the basement, a group of Looney's team sat around, smoking blunt after blunt. When the group noticed the two young boys, they began to clown them.

"What the hell y'all young asses doing in here? Ain't it past y'all bedtime?" Looney's right hand, Joker, joked.

Day'onne scowled at Joker, causing him to taunt them even more.

"Am I supposed to be scared of you? Take y'all little asses home!"

Day'onne and Menace ignored him as Looney led them to a nearby corner. Lifting up an orange milk crate and placing it onto a table, he sorted through the crate before pulling out several .9mm handguns.

"Pick which ones y'all like," Looney said before backing away.

Day'onne studied each gun, focusing on the structure and style of them. Staring at a gold-plated .9mm that had an "L" carved on the handle, he picked it up. He instantly fell in love with the feeling of the heavy metal in his hands.

He knew with that gun, he'd have more power over people's lives than he did before.

"I want this one," he said firmly.

"You think you can handle that, boy?" Looney joked.

Eyeing him with a frown and a demonic look on his face, Day'onne remained quiet and nodded.

"Alright, that'll be a buck. You take care of that. I only had one like that," Looney said, taking the money out of Day'onne's hands.

Menace, on the other hand, chose a black-and-chrome .9mm with a silencer attachment. After paying Looney, the two boys were on their way.

✠ ✠ ✠

A couple of days later, Day'onne and Menace stood in Menace's living room, dressed in all black and each carried a duffle bag. That night, they were on their first mission. They had spent the last two weeks plotting against a drug lord in Pittsburgh that went by the name of Jewels.

Jewels was a major drug dealer in the game and had been in the

industry for over a decade. If they got away with robbing him, they'd have more than enough money and drugs to start their new careers as drug dealers.

"You ready, bro?" Menace asked, twisting the silencer onto his gun.

Day'onne nodded, placing his gun into the pocket of his hoodie.

"Yeah, remember, Menace, this dude is not like the ones we usually rob. We have to be in and out. Shoot now, ask questions later, okay?"

"I already know, let's do this."

Walking out of Menace's apartment, Day'onne and Menace went over their plan one last time before disappearing into the night. They walked up Penfort Street and placed their hoods over their heads. It was three in the morning and the street corners were still filled with hungry hustlers. Some hustlers were shutting down for the night, while others were just opening. Day'onne watched as a pearl-white BMW pulled up by them and a brown-skinned woman climbed out of it and staggered into the street and yelled obscenities to no one in particular. She had on a dirty, skimpy dress that hung loosely off of her gaunt body. As they walked closer to the woman, she looked straight into Day'onne's eyes, causing his heart to get caught into his throat.

Noticing the familiar light, slanted eyes on the woman, he realized that it couldn't be anyone else other than his biological mother.

"Hey, baby, want to have a good time tonight? I'll suck your dick," Relisha said in a drunken slur.

Reaching into the pocket of his hoodie and grabbing a hold of his gun, he clutched it as he tried his best to fight back his tears.

Even though he'd never seen his biological mother a day in his life, this woman before him had to be her. He'd heard stories of his mother being not only a cocaine addict, but also a prostitute.

And from the seldom nervous feeling that arose from within, Day'onne knew this was the infamous Relisha.

He clenched down on his jaw, trying to suppress his anger. It took all the strength in his body for him not to pull out his gun and shoot her.

"Get the fuck out of here you, dirty bitch!" Menace spat harshly.

"Well, forget y'all too, then!" she yelled as she turned and walked away.

Day'onne continued to walk toward his destination with Menace following behind him. He wanted to run the opposite way and fall into Relisha's arms and cry, but with a glare on his face and too much pride in his heart, he gritted his teeth as he turned his attention back to the task at hand.

As they walked toward one of Jewels' major drug houses, he looked over at Menace and said, "Here we go, bro. You sure you ready?"

"I was born ready. Let's do this."

As they approached the back door of the house they were targeting, they saw a small group of hustlers dressed in all black, guarding it. Jewels' watchmen stood on high alert and carried huge shotguns, on the lookout for anything suspicious.

Hiding behind a bush, they squatted down and pulled out their guns. Taking a deep breath, Day'onne nodded to Menace before standing to his feet, raising his .9mm and pulling the trigger. When one of the workers fell to the ground, both of them stepped from behind the bushes and continued to fire their weapons.

Caught off-guard by the sudden attack, the small group was too slow to retaliate. The bullets were coming at them fast and each person was dropping like flies.

Day'onne and Menace continued to fire at them until each and every one of them were down. Moving closer to the door, they

looked at the bodies they'd riddled with bullets. Neither felt any remorse as they pumped more bullets into them, making sure they were permanently silenced.

Walking into the drug house, both of them stayed low on their feet with their guns raised.

"Yo, Cash, is that you?" one of Jewels' workers, Vince, asked before taking a long pull of his blunt.

Vince, who'd been one of Jewels' workers for a couple of years, sat at a table smoking and drinking. He was too drunk to notice the two young thugs in front of him. Day'onne aimed his gun at him and pulled the trigger.

Brain matter and blood splattered everywhere on Day'onne and Menace, causing their stomachs to turn. Ignoring the blood, though, they then placed their guns into their hoodies, pulled the duffle bags from over their shoulders, and started to stuff anything they could possibly lay their hands on, into the bags. They packed everything from stacks of money, to cocaine bricks into the duffle bags until they were filled to capacity. Once they were done, they turned to leave until they heard someone running down the basement steps.

"What the fuck is going on, man?" Vince's best friend, Cash, yelled.

Startled by the sudden outburst, Day'onne and Menace threw the duffle bags over their shoulders and ran out of the back door. As Day'onne ran out of the basement, he didn't notice his .9mm fall out of his hoodie's pocket.

Before Cash could grasp the situation, Day'onne and Menace had already disappeared into the hot, summery night.

CHAPTER FIVE

My struggles,

A young black man misunderstood and judged because of the color of my skin.

My struggles,

Build up pain and blinded by rage.

My struggles,

Blind insanity, imagining perfect pictures of my family and I,

But it isn't perfect at all.

My struggles,

The simple understanding of not knowing my struggles,

So you couldn't understand my hunger for success.

My drive.

Determination.

My struggles,

Northview Heights.

The place where I was born and raised.

The place where I endured my hurt.

Pain.

My struggles,

The place where I saw too many things happen beyond my young age.

My struggles,

Northview Heights.

The place where I had millions of memories that could make or break me.

My struggles...

Deion sat at his desk at school, writing in his journal. He reread the short poem he had just written, slightly dissatisfied. He had spent all afternoon trying hard to come up with the best scenario to start a novel, but it was to no avail.

"Mr. Jenkins, what do you have there that is so important for you not to pay attention in class?" Deion's tenth-grade literature teacher, Ms. Younger, asked, folding her arms across her chest and raising her eyebrows.

Deion glanced around the classroom, noticing he was the only student left.

He was so drawn in by his writing, he didn't notice that the bell had rung.

"Oh, I'm sorry, Ms. Younger. I was..."

"Let me take a look at that," she said before grabbing the notebook off of his desk and interrupting him. Deion watched as she silently read the poem to herself. Ms. Younger was a Caucasian, short woman with piercing blue eyes. She had long brown hair that was cut into professional layers. As she delicately held his notebook in her hands, like it was an infant, he continued to gaze at her, loving the sight of her smooth, white skin.

When she closed his notebook, he asked with concern, "What? You don't like it?"

Remaining silent, Ms. Younger bent down next to him, wrapped her arms around his shoulders, giving him a hug. "Wow, Mr. Jenkins! You have a gift! Where did you learn how to write like that?"

Side-eyeing her, he skeptically replied, "I don't know. But you really liked it?"

"Yes! You need a bit of work and practice, but you're definitely on your way. I'm very impressed, Deion."

Her words caused him to flash a bright smile.

"Thank you. I'm trying to write a book, but I can't. It's too hard." He shrugged.

Stepping in front of his desk and kneeling down, she grabbed Deion by his arm and glanced into his eyes. "Never say you can't do something, young man. You can do it. I refuse to believe that the sky is the limit when there are footprints on the moon. Deion, God has blessed you with an amazing gift and in due time, you can let the world know. For you to be this young and writing like this, imagine how talented you'll be years from now."

"You're right but where do I begin, Ms. Younger? How can I write a book?"

Tapping her freshly manicured nails against her slim chin, she snapped her fingers. "If you stay three days a week after school, I can help you."

Nodding, he stood up and thanked her.

"You have to promise me a few things, Deion."

"What's that?"

"That you'll try your best and don't let that brother of yours influence your decisions."

"I promise, Ms. Younger. I promise," he said before walking out of the classroom.

When Deion walked into the cafeteria, he pulled out his music player, plugged his headphones into his ears and got lost in the ballistic lyrics Tupac spat to him. He bobbed his head to the music as he opened his notebook and went to work. He wrote and wrote and wrote.

The loud, obnoxious teenagers around him didn't faze him at all. He blocked out his surroundings and got lost into the imaginary world of his writing, making love to the paper with his pen. He allowed all of the pain he had built up in his heart to pour out onto the paper. Just as he was finishing his poem, he felt someone tap him on his back.

"What's up, bro?" sixteen-year-old Jarell asked as he took a seat next to him.

Taking the headphones out of his ears, he gave him a hand dap. Jarell, who was a light-skinned kid, was the only person Deion talked to in and out of school. Like Deion, Jarell had been born and raised in Northview and had his own life story behind it. In many ways, Deion and Jarell were alike but Jarell, on the other hand, sold drugs.

"Nothing; what's up with you, though? Still working those blocks?" Deion chuckled.

"Yeah, you know. I got to get this money, my man. That's what you need to be doing, too, instead of walking around here wearing them same basketball shorts and T-shirts."

Ever since they'd met two years prior, Jarell had been trying his best to get Deion to start hustling, but he'd refused.

"Man, how long have you been trying to get me to hustle? You know I can't do that."

"Shit, I don't see why not, bro. Look at what I got on, and look at you," Jarell said before pointing at Deion's usual wardrobe.

Jarell, who was dressed in a pair of crisp Levi's jeans, all-black Chuck Taylor sneakers, and an all-black Levi's shirt, was dressed to impress. Though he made enough money to help his mother with the bills, he always made sure he set enough money to the side occasionally for him to put nice clothing on his own back.

"Nope, I'm good," Deion said nonchalantly.

"I'm not gon' give up on asking you, so be prepared." He laughed before getting up to leave.

As Deion watched Jarell walk away, he couldn't help but think of the day they'd first met two years ago…

It was a cold, winter night and thirteen-year-old Deion walked through the neighborhood, his head held low and tears seeping down his face. He was dressed in a thick leather jacket, a pair of blue jeans, and a long-sleeved thermal shirt. The only things that were missing were his shoes. He placed his hands over the fresh scratches that decorated his face as he continued to walk home. Nervous and feeling defeated, he noticed a light-skinned boy on the corner of Hazlet Street staring a hole through him. He continued to walk with his head held low, praying to God that the boy wouldn't jump on him, either.

"Yo, come here!" the young boy said, waving his hands at Deion.

Deion, who didn't want any trouble, followed his command, quickly walking over to him. He was on the brink of tears as snot fell freely from his nose.

"What's up with you? Where your shoes at, man?" the light-skinned dude asked, glancing at Deion in pure pity.

"They took them," Deion said, in a low, nervous voice.

"Who took them? Why you let them take your shoes?"

"They jumped me and took my shoes!" Deion said, pointing at a group of boys that were down the street.

"Hold up, we gon' get your shoes back."

Gripping his handgun in his pocket, the boy walked behind Deion as he led him to the group of kids that had stolen his shoes. When they approached them, the leader of the crew, Terrence, stepped up to Deion and the light-skinned boy.

"Is there a fucking problem?" Terrence asked, flaring his nose and sticking out his chest.

The light-skinned boy laughed hysterically. He could see right through Terrence's little act.

Pulling out his gun and pointing it directly at Terrence, he said, "Where my homie's shoes at? Who the fuck got his shoes?"

The once rowdy group of boys went completely silent. Terrence's legs buckled as he tried not to urinate on himself.

Quickly kicking the shoes off of his feet, he picked the shoes up off the ground and handed them to Deion. Without warning, the young, light-skinned boy slammed his fist into Terrence's cheek, knocking him to the ground.

"Pick on someone your own fucking size!" he said, spitting on him.

Now grinning from ear to ear, young Deion quickly put his shoes on and said, "Good looking out."

"No worries, I got your back. Don't let these little dudes punk you, man. What's your name?"

"Deion. And yours?"

"They call me Rell, but you can call me Jarell."

When school was finally over, Deion hopped onto the school bus and sat at the front of the bus before plugging his headphones back into his ears. When he noticed a young girl, Shay, get on the bus, his heart almost fluttered. He looked into her gray eyes, hypnotized by her beauty. Shay stood at five-foot-three and was a redbone. She had jet-black, naturally curly hair that she usually wore in a slick ponytail. With her mesmerizing dark gray eyes, bodacious physique, and fierce personality, Shay had a lot of boys wrapped around her young fingers.

She took a seat across from Deion and he tried his best to muster up the courage to talk to her, but he couldn't. She only went for the hustlers, who were pushing luxury cars, reeked of money, and fancy homes—none of which Deion had.

Removing his headphones from his ears, he discreetly eavesdropped on Shay and her best friend, Cherry's, conversation.

"Yeah, girl, you know somebody robbed Jewels' stash spot yesterday?" Cherry said before running her hands through her red hair.

"Jewels? That dude paid! Who robbed him, though?"

Shrugging her shoulders, Cherry replied, "I don't know. But word is Jewels got some change on their heads."

"Whoever did it is bold as hell!" Shay laughed. "Shit, speaking of Jewels, I meant to get his number a minute ago."

"You sick, girl. He's old enough to be your dad!" Cherry said, shaking her head in disbelief.

"Oh well! Got to get it how I live!"

Deion plugged his headphones back in, soaking up all the information he'd heard.

From the nervous feeling that arose in his stomach, he figured something wasn't right. But little did he know, he'd soon find out.

✠✠✠

"Alright, we got over fifty grand in cash, and a hundred grand worth of cocaine-bricks," Menace said before placing the money back into the duffle bags.

The duo was posted up in Deion and Day'onne's bedroom, counting the money they'd stolen from Jewels two nights prior. Ever since they'd murdered Jewels' workers and robbed him, they had stayed low-key. The streets were already buzzing about the robbery and they'd heard about the hit Jewels had on the perpetrators' heads.

"Alright, so where do we begin with this shit? We cooking this

up, bagging it, and selling it ourselves? Or are we getting us a little team we can trust?" Day'onne asked.

"And where the fuck can we find us a team? We only got each other. We can't trust anyone with this shit. We hot as hell! We robbed this dude blind; we can't trust anyone!" Menace growled.

Day'onne nodded his head.

He knew they had to find a way to start up shop on the block, gain some drug addicts, and finally start making that real money by themselves.

"Well, then—"

"Where did y'all get all this money?" Deion asked, barging into the bedroom and interrupting their conversation.

Day'onne and Menace looked up at Deion, scowling at him before placing the rest of the product into the duffle bags and pushing it under Day'onne's bed.

"Mind your fucking business," Day'onne spat, standing up.

"What do you mean, mind my business? Where the hell you get all that money from? I hope y'all didn't go out there and rob anybody!" Deion barked.

Menace laughed as he looked Deion up and down. He didn't have any respect for Deion. He thought he was soft. Deion wasn't cold-hearted like the two of them and he didn't like it at all.

"Man, don't your soft ass got homework to do? Why you worried about us?" Menace asked.

"At least I'm in school, with y'all dumb-asses. Now, answer my question, man. Where y'all get that money from?"

"Nigga, don't be coming up in here asking questions and shit. Mind your fucking business like we told you," Day'onne said, fixing his nose up in disgust.

Shaking his head in disbelief, Deion ran out of the room in frustration.

"Why your brother such a bitch?"

"Man, fuck him. But anyway, back to this money talk. When and where we gon' set up shop?"

"We'll figure that out soon," Menace said. "Let's worry about laying low for a while, now. We hot, so we got to watch our every move, understand?"

"Yeah, you right," Day'onne said, nodding. He snapped his finger as if he had a sudden thought. "Aye, did you see my gun?"

CHAPTER SIX

Thirty-year-old Jewels Mitchell stared out the oversized window of the club he owned, Club 412, taking a long pull from his Cuban cigar. He was dressed in an all-black Armani double-breasted designer suit with gray cuff links. His face and head were neatly shaven to perfection, giving him a clean, professional look. With his round, stocky build and dark, black-blue skin, people always jokingly called him the Notorious B.I.G., even though his reputation was much bigger. Jewels had been in the drug game for over a decade now, and he'd seen and done more things than he could remember. Even though he came from a family of hustlers, he not only had more power than the rest of them, but he was also smarter.

When he was around the age of sixteen, he watched his own father get murdered right in front of his very young eyes.

Jewels' father, Mitch, was a drug kingpin back in the '70s, when the drug game was really on the rise. Mitch had taught Jewels everything he knew about this industry at the tender age of ten, which made Jewels not only intelligent, but also quick on his feet. As he got older and wiser, he stayed in the shadows, watching everyone's moves and mistakes, silently learning from them. He wanted to make sure when he stepped in the game, he was always two steps ahead of the next man. By the time he was twenty years old, he and his right hand, Respect, started to sell drugs. They

had their own team, consisting of two other people, Loyal and Wise, and did their own thing. Jewels wanted to make sure he kept his team small; the more intimate his circle was the better.

He'd seen too many people end up either dead or behind bars from having big circles and having that one disloyal member. With his small team, he was fine. As he got older and the game got deeper, he found himself not needing to work the blocks. By the time he was twenty-three, he had touched over a million dollars.

He invested in a club that sat in the heart of Downtown Pittsburgh, naming it Club 412. When he turned twenty-five, he had his team work for him, allowing them to keep money in their pockets and food in not only their mouths, but also their families'. He tried his best to be seldom seen or heard, by any means necessary.

"Did any of you find any info on who did this?" Jewels finally asked, turning to face his team.

He had called a meeting with his small partners on the particular events that had taken place two nights earlier. Ever since he had gotten the call from Cash, about someone not only robbing him, but killing his watchmen, too, Jewels was appalled.

Not once, since stepping into the game, had someone been this bold to rob and kill his workers. Granted, people tried to step to him before, but after making an example out of a couple of people back in the day, many people knew what time it was when it came down to Jewels. The events that had taken place a couple days ago were the most horrendous in all of his years of hustling.

There in the middle of his office sat Loyal, Wise, and Respect, the same people who'd come up in the game with Jewels.

"Nope," Wise said, as he started to massage his goatee. "My workers trying their best to find the people that were involved,

but no one doesn't know anything, yet. I still can't believe somebody was brazen enough to do this. Now we got to bury all of these workers and send their mothers black dresses."

"They still don't got word on who did it, but they did find a gun in the basement," Respect said in his low, raspy voice.

Respect, who was a light-skinned, handsome older man who resembled Shemar Moore, sat in his seat, head held high, silently ready for some action. He had sandy brown hair that was cut into a low fade, full lips, and a broad nose.

"A gun? How's that going to help? What you want me to do, take fingerprints?" Jewels spat.

Removing a pair of latex hand gloves from his pockets, Loyal removed the handgun from a briefcase and slid it in front of Respect. Looking at the gold-plated .9mm with an "L" carved on the handle, Jewels shook his head in disbelief.

"No, boss. Who's the only person up the hood that sells guns? And look at that 'L' that's carved into that shit!" Loyal said.

"Isn't it that cat, Looney?" Jewels asked. "Carving shit into a gun? How dumb could these young cats get?"

Wise spoke up. "The only way we'd find out is if we pay Looney a visit."

✠ ✠ ✠

Jewels and Respect cruised through Northview in Jewels' black-on-black Escalade with the tinted windows. As they made their way through Chicago Street, then Hazlet Street, Jewels glanced into his rearview mirror, shaking his head in disbelief. Loyal and Wise, who drove in Loyal's fiery-red Ferrari with the butterfly doors, were attracting too much attention to themselves and Jewels didn't like it. He saw corner boys looking at them in envy

and scandalous females plotting in their heads how to get them in the bedroom and into their pockets. When they finally reached their destination, they parked their cars and hopped out. It was almost like the whole neighborhood had stopped to recognize the legendary Northview Heights Drug Lords, every eye raping them.

All four men, dressed in expensive designer suits, walked down the street, commanding attention. Arriving on Looney's porch, Loyal quickly knocked on the door.

"Who is it?" Looney asked as he walked toward the door.

They remained quiet as they waited for Looney to answer the door.

Peering into the peephole, Looney almost urinated on himself when he saw Jewels and his crew.

What the fuck they want? he thought. Turning to Joker, he said, "Yo, it's Jewels and his little posse!"

"Jewels? Fuck that nigga want?" Joker asked as he started to tremble.

"I don't fucking know! Get your shit together!"

About a minute later, Looney nervously opened the door and flashed a fake smile. Jewels walked into Looney's apartment with the other three quickly following behind him.

"What's up, Jewels? What can I help you with, player?" Looney asked, closing the front door.

Jewels glanced around Looney's place in disgust. The smell of marijuana, sex, and rotten food assaulted their noses as they walked into the kitchen and took a seat with Looney and Joker following after them. Placing his hands onto the table and folding them, Jewels instructed Looney to take a seat across from them.

"Now, Looney, I'm going to ask you a few questions. I only

want honest answers and there won't be any problems, understand?"

Nodding, Looney shifted in his seat as Jewels stared a hole through him.

"You heard about me being robbed and a few of my workers getting killed, right?" Jewels asked, staring Looney directly in his eyes.

"Yeah, I heard."

"Well, one of my workers found this gun in my stash house," he said before glancing at Loyal.

Loyal reached into his pocket and pulled out a glove. Putting it on, he reached into the briefcase and pulled out the gold-plated .9mm with the "L" carved into the handle.

Looney's hands began to shake as sweat trickled down his forehead. "I can explain!"

"Well, get to fucking explaining!" Wise said impatiently.

Looney understood that he would lose a lot of respect in the hood for snitching, but his life depended on it. The gun was clearly one that he'd sold because he carved "L" into all of them.

"Oh shit, that's the gun I sold to young, crazy-ass Day'onne and his friend, Menace!" he yelled, his eyes growing as big as golf balls.

"Day'onne? Who's that?" Loyal asked.

Jewels knew exactly who young Day'onne was. In fact, he'd known Day'onne since he was in diapers.

"Are you lying to me?" Jewels asked calmly yet coldly.

"No, I remember him and his friend came in here like a week ago. Remember, Joker?" Looney asked, glancing at Joker.

"Yeah, I remember that shit. I was high as hell and young blood looked like he was about to kill me after I threw a couple jokes at him." Joker laughed.

Taking a second to soak up all the information he'd learned, Jewels finally nodded his head as he scratched his chin.

"Alright, I believe you for now. I'm going to look into this. But best believe if you lying, I'm coming back for you. And believe me, you don't want that to happen," he calmly said before standing to his feet.

He walked out of Looney's place, trying to gather his thoughts. Getting back into his Escalade, with Respect, he remained quiet the remainder of the ride back to the club.

"Are you going to tell us who this young dude is?" Respect asked as they walked back into Jewels' office.

Reaching into a nearby cabinet and removing a bottle of Vodka from it, he quietly poured himself a small shot. He took a seat in his chair, with his shot glass still in his hand, and finally asked, "Remember Relisha that used to dance here back in the day?"

Squinting his eyes and tapping his hands against his temple, Respect snapped his fingers. "Oh yeah! She used to be fine as hell! That crackhead bitch! What about her?"

"Okay, remember Derrick that used to hustle up Northview back in the day, too? He used to run a couple blocks on the Southside?"

"Yeah, I remember that nigga. Didn't he get murked, though?"

"Yeah, he did, but that's not what I'm getting at," Jewels said as he tossed the drink back.

"So, what you talking about then?"

"You dumb ass, Relisha and Derrick used to mess around. She had twins by that dude. One of those twins is the one that robbed me."

"Oh, shit!" Respect said, snapping his finger. "You know where he's staying at now?"

"Yup, with that woman Melissa on Hazlet. I heard about that

little dude a couple of times. He out here robbing motherfuckers with his little right-hand man. But he done fucked with the wrong one," Jewels said, shaking his head in disbelief.

"So we hitting him up? Him and his right hand?"

Rubbing his chin, Jewels shook his head as he got up. Even though he had workers and could hire someone to take Day'onne out for him, he refused. He wanted to stare Day'onne directly into his eyes while he stole the breath away from his lungs. Day'onne had crossed a huge line and he had to be dealt with.

Jewels didn't only want Day'onne; he wanted everyone that had any relations with Day'onne. So with that thought, he looked at Respect and cleared his throat. "No, I don't want just him. I want his entire family."

CHAPTER SEVEN

"Are you ready, boy?" Ms. Younger asked Deion.

It was four in the afternoon as Deion sat at his desk with a pen and notebook in his hand. Giving Ms. Younger his undivided attention, he nodded.

"Okay, first thing you need to know about writing a book is that it takes researching, dedication, and patience."

"What do you mean, it takes patience? What if I want them to read my book a couple of months from now? I don't have patience!" he fussed.

"Deion, you can't write a book in one month; it truly takes time. Don't put a time limit on it and don't rush it. If you rush it, your work will never be good. So remember, patience is the key."

Deion nodded, taking note of what she said.

"Next, when you're writing a book, you want your readers to feel the characters' emotions but not by telling them how the character is feeling."

"What do you mean by that?"

"For an example, if you're writing about a rainy, dark day, you'd say, the day was dark and dull, and lacking of life, God's scornful cries falling from the sky."

"So, I would say that instead of simply saying it was raining outside?" Deion asked, raising his eyebrows.

"Exactly! Like I said, that'll get your reader to feel it!"

Deion continued to listen closely to every word of advice she offered him.

"Okay, next lesson, when you're writing a book, you want the words to flow and not force them."

"How can I do that?"

"Simply by letting the words come to you. The last thing you want to do is force your words. That'll make your book weak and your readers will feel cheated."

"Cheated? How could they feel cheated? It's not like they'll know if I forced the words or not!"

Placing her hands on her hips, Ms. Younger scowled at him. "I'm telling you, yes, they will. You want the readers to love and appreciate your writing, not feel cheated and never want to read your work again. What genre are you aiming for?"

"Urban fiction."

"Urban fiction? Oh, you'll definitely need to work hard on that genre. I read a couple of books in that genre, so you'll need to be different and not cliché."

Deion continued to jot down everything Ms. Younger was schooling him on. When an hour passed and he was ready to go, he packed his notebook and pen into his backpack and started to walk out of the room.

"Ehh, Mr. Jenkins, I want to talk to you about one more thing before you go," Ms. Younger said as she removed her glasses.

Walking back over to her, he stood in front of her. "Deion, you're a very intelligent young man and I really want the best for you."

"I know you do, Ms. Younger, and I'm very thankful."

"Well, that's good to know. But I really hope you don't let these young, ignorant teenagers around you influence your decisions in life. You can really go somewhere with this writing, Mr. Jenkins. You're really blessed. When you go home every night, I

want you to keep a journal and write out your thoughts. Every writer writes every day, or at least thinks about writing. You're a writer, keep your head up, and I hope you heed my advice."

Deion nodded his head as he thanked her one last time and walked out of her classroom.

✠ ✠ ✠

"Hey, Momma," Deion said as he wrapped his arms around Melissa's shoulders, giving her a tight hug and kiss on the cheek.

"Hey, baby. How was school?"

"It was good. Ms. Younger is teaching me how to write a book!"

"Write a book? I didn't know you write, baby. Why didn't you tell me?" Melissa asked, a hint of hurt evident in her voice.

"Because you've been tired and stressed a lot lately. I wanted to give you your space, Momma. I'm sorry."

"It's okay, baby. Can I see some of your writing?"

Reaching into his backpack, he pulled out his journal where he kept his poems and gave it to Melissa.

Flipping to the first page, Melissa began to read his poem, "Never Say Never."

Never say Never,
When you pictured yourself being alone in this cold, heartless world,
And you said you'd never would.
Never say never,
When you find yourself working the blocks to feed your family,
When you said you'd never would.
Never say never,
When you see your lady friend doing anything, willingly, to let any man deep in,

and you'd said you never stoop that low,
but you turn around, your skirt's pulled around your ankles.
Never say never,
When you'd said you'd never hurt the woman of your dreams for the woman for the night,
But lift the covers up, your woman sees you cheating.
Never say Never.............

Placing a hand to her chest, Melissa smiled at Deion and pulled him into a warm hug.

"Boy, this is talent. This is a start! I'm happy for you, baby!"

"Thank you, Momma. But that poem is old. I wrote this when I first started to write."

"Baby, I don't care; that was beautiful. I'm so proud of you!"

"Thank you. Did you buy any food yet? And where's Corrine?"

"Yeah, there's food in there, and she's in the room sleep," Melissa said before getting up to head into the kitchen.

She held the notebook in her hand, skimming through the poems he'd written. She was truly happy to see that he was doing something positive with his life.

"Deion, I want you to listen to me," Melissa stated firmly, as she cupped her hands around his face.

"Yes, Momma?"

"I want you to promise me, no matter what happens, that you'll never let anyone take your dreams from you, baby. I want you to promise me that you'll never let that cold-hearted, ignorant brother of yours take your dreams, or influence you to do something you really don't want to do. Please, baby, promise me?"

Nodding, he smiled as he said, "I promise."

✠ ✠ ✠

Day'onne and Menace stood on the corner of Chicago Street, selling product to several drug addicts, who stood in line. For the past two weeks, both boys had been breaking down, cooking, bagging, and selling the product that they'd stolen from Jewels. The cocaine was pure, fresh from the Cubans, and the addicts wanted more and more, making Day'onne and Menace's pockets heavier and heavier. In the short amount of time they'd been selling, both boys had made more than twenty thousand dollars apiece.

Day'onne's hair was twisted to perfection and his pockets were swollen. Dressed in a fresh pair of black-and-gray Adidas, baggy cargo shorts, and a black Ralph Lauren collared shirt, he rubbed his hands together and licked his lips. Menace, on the other hand, wore crisp white Pumas, khaki cargo pants, and an all-white Lacoste collared shirt. His usually matted hair was now cut into a temple fade, giving him a clean-cut look.

Ever since their transformation had taken place, most of Northview had taken heed.

"Hey, Day'onne," a young girl named Philicia said, smiling from ear to ear.

Philicia and her best friend, Tamika, stood in front of Day'onne and Menace, dressed scantily in short shorts and belly shirts. The skimpy outfits exposed their stacked physiques, causing Day'onne's and Menace's mouths to water.

"What's up, ma?" Day'onne asked as he bit his lip.

"What y'all getting into today?"

"Let's cut to the chase; fuck the bullshit, girl. Are we fucking?" Menace bluntly asked Tamika.

Without hesitation, she smiled and held out her hand, allowing him to take it. He licked his lips and walked her into his apartment, with Day'onne and Philicia following after them. Philicia

and Tamika tried to mask their disappointment when they walked into Menace's dirty, roach-infested house.

"Manny, who the hell is these hood rats?" Sharonda, his mother, yelled, addressing him by his birth name.

She was sprawled out on the sofa, naked and sniffing her daily drugs, which only angered him.

"Get the fuck out of here, you nasty bitch!" he spat coldly, grabbing her by her hair and dragging her out of the house.

She wailed out a loud scream as she kicked and clawed at him. When he finally had her out of the house, he went back to doing his business.

"My bad about that, but y'all ready?"

Philicia and Tamika looked at each other and nodded. Troy, Menace's younger brother, wasn't home, so Day'onne took Philicia into his room, while Menace took Tamika into his room and grabbed her by her shoulders and aggressively started to undress her.

"Calm down, boy! You acting like you never got no pussy before!" Tamika yelled.

Menace, who was a virgin, ignored her as he pulled down his shorts and boxers.

"Wait, where the condom at?" she asked, placing her hand on his chest.

"I don't have one." He shrugged as he laid her on his bed and positioned himself in between her legs.

"Wait, dude! No glove, no love!"

He ignored her, grabbed the base of his penis and entered her. She moaned as a wave of pain and pleasure gripped her with each stroke. His eyes rolled to the back of his head as he experienced the first feeling of sex.

"Oh, shit!" he yelled, ejaculating into her.

She twisted her mouth up in disgust as he collapsed on top of her with his chest heaving in and out.

"Damn, that's it? Where's my money?" she asked, holding out her hand.

"Money? What money?" he asked, confused.

"It cost money to beat up on this pussy. That'll be three hundred."

He shook his head, bursting out in loud, hysterical laughter. "Bitch, you done lost your last mind. Get the fuck out of here!" he said, grabbing her by her hair.

She cried as he pulled her out of his bedroom by her long hair. Hearing her loud screams, Philicia came running out of the other room.

"What's going on?" she asked, pulling up her pants.

"You and this bitch done lost y'all fucking minds if y'all think we're paying y'all to fuck. Both of y'all, get the fuck out my spot!" Menace barked.

Philicia quickly buttoned her pants and ran out the front door, behind Tamika.

Day'onne, who sat in Troy's bed with a stiff-on, shook his head in frustration as he got up to leave, too.

"Where you going?" Menace asked.

"Getting me some fucking pussy! I'll be back!"

Ten minutes later, Day'onne walked into his house.

He checked each room, making sure there wasn't anyone home except for Corrine.

When he was sure she was the only one in the house, he walked into her bedroom. Corrine, who was sound asleep, awoke from the sounds of the floor creaking. She clutched her teddy bear tightly as she looked into Day'onne's coal eyes.

"Please don't do this," Corrine cried.

Day'onne ignored her as he began to undress and climbed in

the bed with her. She lay on top of her twin-sized mattress, eyes closed tightly and trembling in fear. She felt his cold hands grip at her ankles before forcefully spreading her legs apart. He yanked her Barbie gown above her waist and ripped her underwear off.

Her legs shook as she tried to remain calm. She held her hands between her legs, struggling to control her bladder. But before she knew it, it got the best of her, and she peed on herself.

"You nasty bitch," Day'onne said, backhanding her.

Tears tumbled down her cheeks as her face jerked forcefully to the left.

Day'onne ignored her cries and cupped his hands over her mouth, muffling her screams. He positioned himself between her legs and forcefully penetrated her.

Corrine released a low, painful moan as she shifted under him and tried to kick him off of her, but it was to no avail. He held her arms over her head and continued to rape her.

His face was the mask of a demon as he stared into her eyes, loving the pain he brought with each violating stroke. She closed her eyes tightly, avoiding eye contact. Realizing once again that her struggling and cries wouldn't save her, all the fight she had left in her body evaporated. She withdrew into herself and imagined she was somewhere else.

When he finished, he leaned over and whispered into her ear. "You know you enjoyed that shit, you dirty hoe. Remember what I always told you, you ain't shit but a hoe."

He collapsed on top of her small body and lay there for a few minutes, trying to catch his breath. Silent and in pain, she watched her brother climb off of her, put his clothes back on, and calmly walk out of her bedroom.

She curled into a fetal position as an agonizing scream escaped from her lips. A few minutes later, she collected all of the

strength she had within and climbed out of her bed. Stepping out of her bloody pajama dress, she threw it into the closet and grabbed a towel before wrapping it around her. Painfully walking out of her bedroom and into the bathroom, she winced in pain with every step she took and closed the door behind her.

Unwrapping the towel from around herself and turning the sink on, she dampened it before taking a bar of soap and lathering the towel. A slew of tears cascaded down her cheeks as she spread her legs and rubbed the damp cloth between them. Her chest heaving with sobs, she turned the sink off, wrapped the towel back around her body, and walked out of the bathroom.

"What happened to you?" Deion asked when she came out.

Deion, who'd just gotten back from playing basketball with Jarell, heard her crying in the bathroom as he was making his way to his bedroom.

When she looked up at him, he saw that she was distraught as he walked closer to her, but she backed away in fear.

"Please don't hurt me, Day'onne!" she cried.

Deion's heart almost broke into pieces as a tear escaped from his eyes. "Corrine, it's me, Deion! What did he do to you, girl?" he asked, wiping his eyes.

Blinded by her tears, her body started to shudder as she collapsed to the floor. Deion walked over, picked her up, and carried her to her room. He felt her tense up when he gently placed her into her bed. When he noticed the blood stains in her bed, he asked, "What happened?"

"He hurt me, Deion. He hurt me down there," she said, pointing at her vagina.

"Why didn't you tell me, Corrine? Why didn't you tell me or Melissa?" he asked as he clenched his jaw.

"He said he'll kill me! Please don't tell Momma! Please, he's

going to kill me!" she yelled in fear before grabbing Deion by his arm and shaking it.

He took a deep breath, digesting everything she'd confessed to him. "I have to tell! He's going to keep hurting you if I don't!"

"But he said he'll kill me. Please don't tell!"

Blinded by anger, he balled his hands into tight fists before punching numerous holes into the wall, instantly drawing blood.

Corrine's loud screams brought him back to reality.

"Stop! Please stop!" she cried, wrapping her arms around her head and burying her face into her lap.

He dropped his head into his hands before walking back to Corrine.

"You can't tell, Deion! He'll kill me. Please promise," she cried.

Taking a deep breath and mustering all the strength he had in his body, he nodded. "Okay, I won't tell. I promise."

Reaching out her hand, she said, "Pinky swear?"

"Pinky swear," Deion said, wrapping his pinky finger around hers.

CHAPTER EIGHT

Melissa arrived at Asbury Heights Nursing Home Facility in Bower Hill, Pennsylvania around three in the afternoon. She wore a floral, ankle-length dress with a pink cardigan sweater. Stepping out of her old station wagon, she took a deep breath as she walked inside and signed in.

When she finally made her way to her mother's front door, she paused to mentally and physically prepare herself for what was behind it. Her mother, Yolanda, who was battling liver cancer, gazed up at Melissa as she walked through the door. Melissa scanned the room, looking at pictures of her and her mother when she was younger. When her eyes roamed to her mother, her lips quivered and hands trembled as she scooted up a nearby chair next to her bed.

"Hey, Momma."

Yolanda tried her best to smile, but it was to no avail. She was in too much pain.

"How are you? Everything's good at home. The twins are getting bigger and so is Corrine. Corrine is beautiful. Remember Corrine?"

Yolanda nodded and Melissa continued, "Momma, I'm trying my best to keep you in here and take care of the kids. It's getting hard, it really is. With crazy Day'onne out here robbing everybody and their momma, to the government trying to cut my welfare checks, it's getting hard, Momma!"

"Pray, baby," Yolanda said, her voice barely a whisper.

"Pray? But Momma, I do that all the time! I can't take it! I'm getting too old for this, Momma! I can't take it!" Melissa said before dropping her head into her hands and crying.

All of her life, she'd helped people, putting their needs before hers, and it was finally getting to her. She never had a real man in her life and never knew what the true feeling of happiness felt like. Since she would be approaching fifty soon, she wanted to finally settle down and be happy, but that was only in her dreams.

Yolanda struggled to speak. "Baby...God is going to bless... you."

Melissa slowly lifted her head up to look into her mother's eyes.

"He loves you, baby. Keep your faith."

Taking heed of her mother's words, she wiped her tears and forced herself to smile. Yolanda, who had been battling the deadly disease for two years, weakly held her daughter's hand. If anyone recognized pain, it was definitely her.

She had been raised in poverty and tried her best to keep her faith and belief in God through all of the trials and tribulations she'd gone through in this cruel world.

Raped by her father and abused by her mother all of her life, Yolanda had done whatever it took to survive in the streets of Pittsburgh. When she got pregnant at sixteen by a man she had sex with one night, who later disappeared, her mother kicked her out of her house, forcing her to live in the streets. While she was pregnant with Melissa, she prostituted her body in order to save up enough money to get her a house. When a friend of the family finally agreed to rent her a house up Northview, she felt blessed. When Melissa was born, she raised her daughter the right way, making sure she always had respect for not only herself, but for other people, too.

Looking at Yolanda, Melissa couldn't help but think that the clock was ticking. Every day, she got a call from the nursing home, alerting her that Yolanda's health was steadily decreasing. When she was finally ready to leave, she kissed her mother goodbye.

When Melissa arrived back up Northview, in a much better mood, she was smiling and feeling good. Pulling her keys from her purse, she unlocked her door and stepped into her apartment. Finding it unusually dark and cold, she felt uneasy.

"Twins? Corrine?" she yelled, but no one answered.

As she walked toward the light switch to turn on the light, a pair of large, beastly hands wrapped around her slim neck.

"Where's the rest of them at?" Jewels asked, staring into Melissa's eyes.

Fear gripped her as she gasped for air. When he let go of her neck and tossed her onto the sofa, she coughed uncontrollably and tears streamed from her eyes. She sat on the couch, trying to catch her breath and grasp the whole situation.

"Why are you here? What do you want?" she asked, her voice trembling.

"Your boy got himself into some trouble, and now he has to pay the price. Where the fuck is he at?" Jewels asked impatiently.

"I don't know! I just got here! Please don't hurt my babies!" Melissa cried.

"I'm sorry, Melissa, but he's played a dangerous game and he has to pay the price."

"What do you—"

Before Melissa had a chance to utter another word, Jewels lifted his .45 caliber, aimed it at her chest and pulled the trigger. The bullet ripped right through her heart, instantly killing her.

✠ ✠ ✠

Deion and Corrine sat in the front pew of the church in Brighton Heights, bawling their eyes out. It had been more than a week since the death of Melissa, and she was finally being laid to rest. Dressed in a long, black dress with red flowers that Melissa had bought her a long time ago and her hair flat-ironed, Corrine held Deion's hand, weeping and sniffling up the snot that was threatening to seep out of her nose. Deion, who was dressed in an all-black suit, shook his head in disbelief as he prayed to God to send the only mother he'd ever known back to him. The church was filled to capacity, the majority of different communities in the city coming together to pay their last respects to Melissa. She had undoubtedly made a special impact on everyone's lives that showed their faces in the church. Melissa, who was being laid to rest in her favorite lime-green cardigan sweater and ankle-length skirt, appeared peaceful in the silver-plated casket.

"Where's Day'onne?" Melissa's neighbor whispered into Deion's ear.

Deion shrugged, instantly angered by the mention of Day'onne's name.

Something in the pit of his soul told him that Day'onne was the reason his mother was no longer breathing. Anything from him having stacks of money in the duffle bags to him wreaking havoc on the entire Northview could've made someone yearn to take Melissa's life.

When the preacher finally delivered the eulogy and the crowd made its way to dinner, Deion grabbed Corrine by the hand and walked toward the casket. He mentally tried to prepare himself to get one last look at his hero, but when he looked at Melissa, seeing the serene look on her face, he wanted to break down and cry.

Corrine, who couldn't take it anymore, collapsed into his arms,

her body shaking before she released a loud, mournful cry. He tried his best to keep his composure, but he also collapsed onto the floor, wailing out tears of pure anguish. They felt as if without Melissa, they didn't have anybody but themselves.

"Come on, baby girl, we got to get it together," Deion whispered into Corrine's ear as he wiped his tears away and stood up.

She nodded as he she stood as well. Walking toward the front entrance of the church, they noticed an older white woman with a policeman behind her.

"Hello, are you Corrine Johnson and Deion Jenkins?" she asked.

"Who wants to know?" Deion asked cautiously.

"I'm Diane Puchiarelli from Child Protective Services. Both of you need to come with me. Isn't there another one?"

The mention of CPS panicked Deion. Without hesitation, he grabbed Corrine by the arms and raced past Ms. Puchiarelli and the policeman. Both turned around and took off after them. Fleeing the church and hitting the corner, Deion and Corrine stopped and glanced around when several policemen surrounded them.

Turning around, Deion saw Ms. Puchiarelli behind him. "Run, Corrine!" he yelled, releasing her hand. But it was too late. Ms. Puchiarelli already had the little girl in her arms, ready to take her away.

CHAPTER NINE
EIGHT YEARS LATER...

"Corrine, hurry up! You're going to get us caught," sixteen-year-old Mercedes fussed.

She nervously glanced around the Giant Eagle grocery store, making sure no one was aware of their activities. Corrine ignored Mercedes as she continued to carelessly throw any type of food she laid her eyes on into the duffle bag draped around her waist. Mercedes' heart slammed into her chest when she saw an employee speaking into a walkie-talkie, alerting his boss that two teenagers were shoplifting.

"C'mon, Corrine, we got to get out of here!" she yelled, grabbing Corrine by the wrist.

Both teens ran through the aisles, trying to get out of the grocery store without being caught.

"Aye, stop right now!" one of the store managers yelled as he ran after them.

Corrine looked behind her and saw he was right on her heels.

"He's coming!" she yelled, clutching the duffle bag full of food even tighter.

They were almost out the door when she was tackled to the ground. She moaned in pain as the fat manager grabbed her by her arms, forcing her to her feet.

Mercedes, who was already out of the door, glanced behind her and realized Corrine wasn't there. When she ran back into the store, she saw the manager leading her into a back room.

"Hold up; it was me, too!" she yelled, getting the manager's attention. "I stole the food as well!"

Corrine flashed a smile at her best friend as the manager led them both into the back room. Taking the duffle bag out of Corrine's hand, the manager frowned as he dumped the food onto a nearby table. Corrine and Mercedes sat next to each other, holding their heads low as he called the police.

"What do you two have to say for yourselves?" he finally asked.

He looked at the two rough-looking teens, feeling both pity and animosity toward them at the same time. He would not tolerate theft on his watch. Corrine, who was dressed in a torn and dingy white T-shirt, skimpy blue jean shorts, and had on a pair of torn Reebok Classics, sat in the chair with her arms crossed under her breasts, staring up at the ceiling.

She inhaled air, puffing out her cheeks as she moved her eyes, glancing at one side of the room and then the other. Sighing, she began to tap her foot impatiently.

Mercedes, who was dressed in a pair of ripped-up jeans, a faded black shirt, and torn tennis shoes, sat in the seat, shaking her leg, glancing around the room, and running her fingers through her hair.

"We're sorry, sir. Please let us go. We promise we won't do it again!" she begged, a single tear trickling down her cheek.

"I'm sorry, young ladies, but if you do the crime, you must do the time." He shrugged.

Twenty minutes later, when a policeman finally arrived, he placed both Corrine and Mercedes in handcuffs before stuffing them into the back of his car.

Feeling humiliated and gripped with embarrassment, tears continued to escape from Mercedes' eyes throughout the entire ride. When they pulled into the parking lot at the police station,

they stepped out of the car and entered into the building. Corrine shrugged as she took a seat and waited patiently for their next punishment.

"What are your names?" a policewoman, Officer Williams, asked, taking a seat in front of the two girls.

"Mer…mer…cedes," she stammered.

Corrine, who had her arms folded under her breasts, rolled her eyes and glanced at Mercedes.

"Okay, Ms. Mercedes, and what is your name?" Officer Williams asked, looking at Corrine.

"Why the fuck you want to know?" Corrine asked.

Officer Williams, a beautiful black woman who wore her hair shortly cropped and had an aura as soft as an angel, stared at Corrine, shaking her head in pity. She already knew their names because they had been printed and run through the system. She was simply trying to make conversation and get them to open up.

Working in her profession for the past five years of her life, she had seen many at-risk teenagers that emulated the ones currently in front of her. Instead of going off and yelling in their faces like the other female officers would've, she remained calm.

She looked Corrine directly into her eyes. "Sweetie, all I want to know is your name. Why all the hostility? I'm here to help you get out of this little sticky situation you two got yourselves into. I can tell them to send you up to Shuman Detention Center for theft and you'd be fined for stealing over three hundred dollars' worth of food, but, instead, I'm going to be nice. So, if you want my help, all I ask for you is to be respectful and honest and I'll return the love."

Corrine exhaled loudly, rolled her eyes, and started tapping her feet again.

"Okay, Ms. Thang, let's try this again. But this time, I want you

to cut the attitude and look me directly into my eyes and tell me your name," Officer Williams said firmly.

Unfolding her arms from her chest and staring Officer Williams directly in her eyes, Corrine snottily said, "My name is Corrine. Are you fucking happy now?"

Shaking her head in disbelief, Officer Williams made a mental note to check her for her profanity later. Deciding to leave the situation alone for now, she flipped through Mercedes' and Corrine's records she'd retrieved moments ago. Taking heed of the petty theft charges from not only stealing groceries, but clothes as well, she silently set their folders down.

She scanned their worn-out clothing, knowing they had to be doing what they were doing to survive.

I know the feeling, she thought, standing to her feet.

"Okay, we called your foster care mother, Rachael, and she'll be here to pick you two up any minute now."

"You told Rachael on us?" Mercedes asked, shifting in her chair.

Noticing the fear in her eyes, Officer Williams sat back down and took her by the hand.

"Yes, we had to, sweetie. Why were y'all out there stealing food when she provides it at the foster home?"

Snatching her hand away from her, tears streamed down Mercedes' cheeks as fear gripped her.

"We don't have anything to eat up there! She treats us like shit! She's going to—"

"Would you shut the fuck up, Mercedes?" Corrine yelled, interrupting her. "You know you're not supposed to say shit to no one. It's not like this bitch cares, anyway. She's like the rest of them!"

Looking at Corrine through distressed eyes, Mercedes nodded in agreement, wiped her tears, and inhaled.

"Your mouth is filthy, Ms. Corrine. How do you know if I would care or not? You don't know me, like I don't know you. Baby girl, I'm only here to help," she assured Corrine.

Before Corrine had a chance to reply, she locked eyes with her foster mother.

Rachael, a white woman dressed in a black blouse and a black knee-length skirt, flashed a fake smile as she walked up to Officer Williams, extending a pale hand.

"Hello, are you the guardian of these two girls?" Officer Williams asked, standing to her feet and shaking Rachael's hand.

"Yes, I am. I'm very sorry for the inconvenience these two have caused; they never seem to stay out of trouble," Rachel said, trying her best to sound professional. "I try my best to raise and do the best I can for these girls, but it's practically useless."

Corrine and Mercedes sucked their teeth as they watched the fake act Rachael performed.

"It's fine, but I'm wondering why they're out here stealing, anyway? They wouldn't be doing it if they didn't have a reason to," Officer Williams said, raising her eyebrows in suspicion.

"There's no reason for them to be foolish." She paused to see if the officer was buying it. "Now, I'd like to be on my way. C'mon, girls," Rachael said in a dismissing tone.

Corrine and Mercedes watched as Rachael walked out of the police station and followed after her. Officer Williams, who felt as if there was more to the story, quickly took out her business card with her email and personal cell phone number and gently grabbed Mercedes by the wrist.

"Please, if you need any help, don't hesitate to call me," she said, placing the card into her hand.

Mercedes nodded, placed the card into their duffle bag and walked out of the station.

✠ ✠ ✠

"Didn't I fucking tell y'all stupid hoes not to get caught?" Rachael yelled at the top of her lungs.

Corrine and Mercedes sat in the corner of the bedroom they shared, their legs wobbling and lips quivering. Rachel, who had fire blazing in her eyes, ignored their cries as she marched out of their room. Walking toward the kitchen, she kicked a pile of trash out of her way. The foul stench of spoiled food assaulted her nose as she walked into the kitchen and removed the scorching hot water that she had started boiling earlier from the stove.

"Mom, I'm hungry!" Rachael's biological daughter, Tessa, cried as she clutched her stomach.

"I don't give a fuck! Blame your sisters for getting caught stealing the fucking food!" she spat harshly as she walked back into the room.

"Run, Corrine!" Mercedes yelled as Rachael walked toward them with the boiling water.

Corrine tried to run past Rachael, but before she had a chance to move her feet, their foster mother threw the water at both of them. Wailing out blood-curdling screams, Corrine and Mercedes collapsed to the ground, wrapping their arms around their now burned flesh. Rachael quickly picked up a belt that had a heavy buckle from off the floor, and started to beat both girls without mercy, causing them to scream louder.

Mercedes tried screaming again, but all that came out was a loud screech.

"Please stop!" she begged, starting to lose consciousness.

Corrine, who was now silent, remained curled up into a ball, numb to the pain. She closed her eyes, imagining she was somewhere else other than the hell-hole she was in.

"Now, I want you black nigger bitches to stay in here and think about what you did. If you come out this room, that's y'all asses!" Rachael warned before slamming the door behind her.

Mercedes winced in pain as she grabbed the bottom of her jail-like mattress bed and pulled herself onto it. Her flesh felt raw and sore with every move she made.

Tears of sorrow tumbled down Corrine's eyes as she rocked herself back and forth. Her long hair was wild and tangled on the top of her head, and her brown, mocha skin was almost beet red. No stranger to the great pain she was enduring, she mustered up the little strength she had left in her fifteen-year-old body and pulled herself through the piles of food, trash, and dead rodents that lay on her bedroom floor.

Lying next to Mercedes in the bed they were forced to share, she wrapped her arms around her best friend and laid her head on her chest, weeping.

"We got to get out of here, Mercedes. I can't take this anymore," she cried, choking over her words.

"I know, Corrine. I know."

✠ ✠ ✠

Mercedes Owens was born and raised in many different areas of the city. Her mother, Theresa Harper, who died while giving birth to Mercedes, planned to give her daughter the life and childhood she never had. Theresa worked as a math teacher at one of the Pittsburgh public schools. She was no stranger to growing up and not having anything she could call her own. Raised by an alcoholic mother, she'd had to learn the hard way of how to make it through life. She fought hard for everything she owned and she tried her best in focusing on her own life

goals. Growing up not knowing her father, she always yearned to feel that love by the other gender.

So when she met Darnell Owens, she quickly fell head over heels for him.

Darnell was a certified womanizer in Pittsburgh. A lot of women fell in love with his charming personality, piercing hazel eyes, light skin, and masculine features. He dipped not only into females' panties, but their pockets, also.

Theresa, who was twenty-five when she met Darnell, met him while she was leaving work one day. She had endured a long day at work and all she wanted to do was go home and get some rest. She walked out of the middle school, her bronze, flawless skin glistening in the sunlight. Her hair was pinned up in a pile of curls, emphasizing her exotic cheekbones and almond-shaped eyes. She was dressed in a royal-blue skirt suit, semi-revealing her curvaceous legs. By the powerful strut of her walk, the perfect curl of her lips, and the way she held her head in confidence as she walked, Darnell was enticed by her.

"Yo, ma! What's up?" he yelled, running across the street.

Turning around to face him, Theresa tried her best to mask her disappointment as she saw the ignorant man before her.

"Well, is that a kind of way to approach a woman? I'm a lady, talk to me like a man is supposed to talk to a woman," she said, folding her arms across her chest.

Taken aback by her response, Darnell knew he'd underestimated the beautiful woman before him. He was so used to scandalous, ghetto females that he didn't recognize a real woman when he saw one.

"I apologize. But my name is Darnell, and yours?"

"Theresa. Theresa Harper; it was nice to meet you," she said, turning and walking toward her car.

"Wait, wait, Theresa! I was wondering if I could take you out sometime, you know? Have a good time together," he said, licking his lips seductively.

Looking into his deep, hazel eyes, Theresa almost melted. He was hard to resist.

It's been four years since I've been with a man, she thought. *He's not the best, but he sure is a start.*

"Okay, that'll be fine; call me later." She wrote down her number and passed it to him.

A couple of days later, after Darnell finally decided to call her, he took her to a fancy restaurant downtown. Overwhelmed with emotion and a little tipsy off the alcohol, Theresa knew she had to have him that night.

That night, he seduced her, taking her body places it had never been before. That night, not only had she caught feelings for him, she had also conceived.

NINE MONTHS LATER...

"C'mon, Darnell! My water broke! Can you meet me at this hospital, please?" Theresa cried into the cell phone as she took short, deep breaths.

Darnell, who was at yet another female's house, sighed. He couldn't care less about Theresa having his child; he already had over six kids.

"Look, I told you I'm busy and I can't make it. Give my daughter a kiss for me. I'll talk to you later," he said, ending the call.

She tossed her cell phone at the hospital wall in complete frustration.

"Okay, Ms. Harper, I need you to calm down and take a deep breath. Your child is on her way now and your blood pressure is very high; that's very dangerous," the doctor warned her.

Theresa's chest heaved in and out and tears blinded her sight. As she lay there, preparing to birth her first child into the world by herself, she regretted even meeting Darnell. She despised him for leaving her at the hospital like that. Six hours and twenty minutes later, she gave birth to a healthy baby girl, naming her Mercedes Owens.

Even though she had mixed emotions about Darnell, she still decided to give her daughter his last name. Theresa only had one chance to look at her daughter's beautiful hazel eyes that she inherited from her father before she had a massive heart attack, dying holding her child.

✠✠✠

As Mercedes got older, she was moved from foster home to foster home, not being able to call any place a real home. Throughout her short sixteen years on earth, she'd been abused mentally, physically, and emotionally. She'd learned a long time ago how cold and callous this world was. Growing up, she never trusted any of the males or females that she had to call her brothers and sisters in the numerous foster homes she traveled through. After a while, she plastered it in her mind that the foster homes she moved through were only temporary. But after being placed to live with an angry, abusive white woman, Rachael Moye, Mercedes found it hard to believe that she'd ever leave that hellhole. Rachael lived in one of the projects on Brighton Ridge and was considered a hustler, adopting random children and using the paychecks she earned from them to get high.

✠✠✠

When Corrine Johnson, who was nine at the time, was sent to live with Rachael, Mercedes was instantly drawn to the young girl. The couple of months there, Mercedes, who was a year older than Corrine, kept Corrine close to her at all times and made sure that Rachael never laid a finger on her. But after a while, Rachael started to abuse both girls without mercy, beating them with anything she could lay her hands on.

"Mercedes?" Corrine cried one night as she stared at the dark walls.

It was her first week living there and one of the worst weeks of her life. That night, high off drugs and with her adrenaline rushing, Rachael had beaten them for almost an hour straight for no given reason.

"Yes, Corrine?" Mercedes asked, her voice trembling.

"Do you ever think about your real family and how your life would've been if you were with them?"

"Yes, I do. I think about it all the time. But I never knew my mother or father. What about you? Did you know your family?"

Taking a deep breath, Corrine nodded. "Yes, my momma died when I was seven. I had two older brothers that are identical twins, too."

Mercedes turned to face her. "Well, at least you knew your family. What was it like having a real family?"

"Well, one brother raped me for about two years, and my favorite brother, Deion, he was so nice and he did anything for me. I miss him so much," Corrine cried.

Placing her hand to her chest, Mercedes replied, "I didn't know you were raped. I'm sorry to hear that, sister."

"It's fine. Only you and Deion know." Corrine shrugged. "And Mercedes?"

"Yes, Corrine?"

"Will you always be my friend and never leave my side?"

Lifting her head up, Mercedes grabbed Corrine's hand. "Yes, I'll always be here for you, Corrine. What made you ask that?"

"Because I'm tired of people walking in and out of my life. I'm tired, Mercedes," Corrine continued to cry.

"Well, you don't have to worry about that anymore, Corrine. Best friends until the end."

"You promise?"

"I promise."

✠✠✠

"Mercedes? Corrine? Are y'all okay?" fourteen-year-old Tessa asked, peeking into their bedroom.

Corrine and Mercedes, who were still in great pain from the brutal beating Rachael had laid on them earlier, groaned in pain as they both turned to face her. Both girls' flesh was still beet red and stiff from the boiling hot water Rachael had thrown at them. Tessa walked into the room with a loaf of bread and a jug of water in her hands. Kneeling, she opened the bread and took two pieces out and turned toward Mercedes. Opening her mouth, she took a piece of the bread, popped it into her mouth, and watched as Mercedes forced herself to chew it. Turning to Corrine, she repeated the same steps and helped them drink out of the jug of water.

When she knew both girls were satisfied, she left the room.

For the next couple of days, Rachael had left Corrine and Mercedes to rot in misery in their tiny, dirty bedroom. The room was filthy. Dead rodents, mouse droppings, and old trash were scattered around. At night, lying on the dirty jail-like bed that was very small and thin, the girls had to deal with the chirping sounds of rats eating at the garbage that was on the floor.

"Are you okay, Mercedes?" Corrine asked in a low, weak voice.

It was three in the afternoon and both girls were curled in a fetal position, gripped with fatigue and hunger. It had been two days since they'd had anything to eat and if they didn't eat quickly, they'd die from starvation. Wincing in pain, Mercedes nodded and bravely stood up. A wave of pain washed over her and her knees buckled as she fell. Corrine struggled to her feet and helped her back up, both their faces masks of pain. Taking small steps, they went to the door, opened it cautiously, and peeked out, remembering Rachael's warning.

They had taken heed to Rachael's warning and were too weak to endure another beating.

When they noticed the small hallway was clear, both girls walked as fast as they could into the kitchen. Mercedes opened the refrigerator, not too disappointed at what she saw. There were a couple of flies circling around a half-empty pot of ravioli and a jug of water.

Taking the ravioli out of the refrigerator and placing it onto a plate, she popped it into the microwave.

"Here, eat this," she said, after removing the plate and passing it to Corrine.

"How about we both eat it?" Corrine asked, picking two forks from off the floor and passing one to Mercedes.

In a matter of seconds, they demolished the ravioli. Looking at the empty plate, their stomachs turned.

"I can't take this shit anymore," Corrine cried, clutching her stomach and falling to the floor.

"Well, we have to deal with it, Corrine. Where else will we go?" Mercedes asked, taking a seat next to her.

"I don't know," Corrine said.

Wrapping her arms around her best friend's shoulders, Mercedes managed to flash a fake smile. "We'll find a way, Corrine. Trust me, we'll find a way."

CHAPTER TEN
PRESENT DAY...

When Deion arrived home from his book signing that night, he couldn't help but think about the conversation he had with Day'onne. His thoughts ran a mile a minute as he walked into his condominium, located on the Southside of Pittsburgh.

"You okay, baby?" Yoka, asked, rubbing his masculine chest.

"Yeah, I'm cool."

Yoka noticed how quiet Deion had been on his way back home. "You look stressed. Can I help take that tension away?" she asked, smiling seductively.

They were seated on his La-Z-Boy chair in his living room. Even though he really didn't want any company at that moment, he could use the stress reliever.

"Give it a shot, baby," he said, flashing a fake smile.

Yoka, who had radiant dark skin, rocked a short haircut, and had a strong resemblance of Naomi Campbell, continued to smile as she slid in between his legs. Unzipping his slacks and pulling them down, she licked her lips as she held his thick penis in her hands.

Teasing the head with the tip of her tongue, she moaned and went to work. Deion closed his eyes and threw his head back as he grabbed the back of her head and moaned. Yoka took a deep breath as she slid his penis deeper and deeper into her mouth until the head was nearly down her throat.

"Alright, alright, come here," he said, standing to his feet.

He reached into his pants pocket, pulling out a Magnum condom and placing it on himself. Lifting Yoka against the wall and wrapping her legs around his waist, he slowly entered her, teasing her opening with the tip of his penis.

She tossed her head back in ecstasy when he was fully inside of her. He held her tight, stroking deeply.

"Harder, harder!" she moaned, biting her lip.

He held her closer, pounded her harder, causing her to have multiple orgasms.

Fifteen minutes later, Deion ejaculated into the condom and collapsed to the floor, holding Yoka in his arms.

✠ ✠ ✠

"Hey, Ms. Younger," Deion said as he walked into Ms. Younger's small duplex.

"Hey, baby, what are you doing here so early?" Ms. Younger asked, glancing at her watch, noting it was only ten in the morning.

"I had a lot on my mind and I needed someone to talk to," he said, taking a seat on her couch.

Ms. Younger, who was still dressed in her nightwear, took her robe off of the couch and put it on. Taking a seat next to her adopted son, she looked at him, seeing the stress in face.

"What's wrong, baby?"

"It's nothing."

"Now you know I've known you for the past decade of your life and I can tell when something's bothering you. So, what is it?"

Taking a deep breath, Deion dropped his face into his hands, shaking his head. "Day'onne showed up to the book release party yesterday."

"What's wrong with that? I know that boy is trouble, but that's still your twin. Y'all are family, Deion."

"It's not that. When he came up to me, he asked me to start working for him. So, then he goes on and says some man named Jewels is about to get out and he'll be looking for us."

"Who's Jewels?" Ms. Younger asked, confused.

"Some old hustler from Northview that used to run it back in the day. Well, he probably still does, but I don't know. I'm confused. What does Jewels want with me, Day'onne, and Corrine? Whatever it is, Day'onne's name is written all over it," Deion spat viciously.

"And what makes you think Day'onne had something to do with this?" she asked, trying to put the pieces together.

"Because, I can just tell. Day'onne isn't nothing but trouble, Ms. Younger. All he does is go around being a menace to society. Whatever it is, though, I want no parts. I got this book to worry about and I don't need any drama."

Wrapping her arms around Deion's shoulder, she gave him a warm hug. "Baby, I understand it's hard for you, but he's still a part of your family. What do you think Ms. Melissa would've wanted you to do?"

The mention of Melissa's name brought him into an even more somber mood. Every time he thought of her, he couldn't help but think about all the things she'd done for him and the unconditional love she'd provided him with.

Pushing her to the back of his mind, he shook his head as he stood up.

"This isn't about Melissa!" he yelled, trying to fight back his tears. "This is about Day'onne entering my life out of nowhere, right when things are finally positive for me. I haven't seen or spoken to him in the past eight years of my life, and now he sud-

denly pops up out of nowhere talking about some old gangster out to get me!"

"Boy, would you calm down?" Ms. Younger said, tapping him on the leg. "Listen, it may be a lot to digest, but you have to calm down, Deion. He is your family. Even when I adopted you following Melissa's death, it seemed like you didn't want anything to do with your family. Why is that? Speaking of family, when was the last time you even talked to Corrine?"

"Since they took her. I tried to locate her, but they couldn't find her," he lied, eyeing the floor.

Standing and shaking her head in disbelief, Ms. Younger said, "I'm highly disappointed in you, Deion. This book means a lot to you and it's your dream, but they are your family. No, you don't have to hustle or get into all of the shenanigans that Day'onne gets himself into. What I'm saying is that you should have their backs and find out why this man is after all of y'all."

"So what should I do, Ms. Younger?"

"I don't know, baby. You're a grown man now, and it's time you make your own decisions. All I can say is follow your heart."

CHAPTER ELEVEN

Rachael sat Indian-style in the middle of her dirty living room floor, going into a head nod. She clutched the crystal meth in her hands, slobber seeping from the corners of her mouth. Her white complexion was ghostly pale from the drugs she'd been taking for more than two years. Her blonde hair that was once flawlessly healthy was now breaking off into chunks, and her pink lips were white and chapped.

She'd been sitting in the living room for hours now, rocking her head back and forth. An hour later, when she felt the drug wearing off, she looked at the small bag of crystal meth she had left in her hand and reached for the needle. As she held the needle in her hand, she heard the faint sounds of Corrine, Mercedes and Tessa, in the next room talking.

Quickly standing and flaring her nose, she tossed the needle down before making her way toward their bedroom.

"Why does your mom treat us like this?" Mercedes asked Tessa.

All three of them were seated in a semi-circle in Corrine and Mercedes' bedroom, having a sister-to-sister talk.

"I don't know; I guess it's the drugs," Tessa said, shrugging her shoulders.

"Man, fuck those drugs! That ain't a reason for her to be fucking us up the way she do! You don't have shit to worry about, Tessa. You don't go through the shit we go through up in here!" Corrine spat, trying to hold back her tears.

"Would you calm down and watch your mouth, Corrine?" Mercedes said, lightly slapping Corrine's arm.

"I don't know. When I was younger, she was the best mother but then..." Tessa paused as she thought back to when Rachel used to bend over backward to make sure she had everything.

"Then what, Tessa?"

"My father up and left one day. I don't know why, but he did. After that, she became depressed and angry. She ended up adopting you, Mercedes, got them checks and it helped feed her habit. When she got on them drugs, it became worse than before."

Corrine and Mercedes watched as a tear made its way down Tessa's cheek. Tessa, who was biracial, was a beautiful young girl who, like Corrine and Mercedes, was misguided and lost in this world. When Rachael had gotten hooked on drugs and lost herself, Tessa had lost herself, too.

"Don't cry, girl," Mercedes said, giving Tessa a hug.

"No, I hate to see her do this to y'all. I don't know why she doesn't hit me, but when she abuses y'all, it feels like she's doing it to me, too. Y'all don't know, I don't have anyone but y'all. I don't want y'all to leave me."

"Girl, don't worry; we're not going anywhere," Corrine assured her.

"I heard y'all talking about it the other day. If y'all leave, I really don't blame you. But please know I'm leaving with y'all."

"We can't leave because we don't know where to go!"

Taking a deep breath and wiping her tears, Tessa tapped her fingers against her chin as if she was thinking. Snapping her fingers, she said, "I have a friend that used to work for some woman name Sugar. She can give us a place to stay."

"Sugar? Who's Sugar?" Mercedes asked skeptically.

"She's a pimp."

"So you saying your friend used to sell her body and that's what you want us to do, too? Oh, hell no!"

"Shit, I'd rather do that than continue to live in these conditions. Sugar is cool. She's not your usual pimp. I won't be in here for long and y'all don't want to be either," Tessa said.

Mercedes took a deep breath, thinking about what Tessa had said. Even though it was hell living with Rachael, she couldn't see herself sinking to a new low by selling her body.

"Think about it, y'all."

"No, but—"

Before Mercedes had a chance to finish her statement, Rachael came barging into their bedroom like a madwoman. Her eyes were blood red and appeared crazed.

"What the fuck y'all doing in here? Tessa, get the fuck out!" she yelled, lunging at Corrine.

Corrine curled into a ball, praying to God, trying to prepare herself for the brutal beating coming her way. Her body was still sore from the beating a few days ago, and she wasn't physically ready for another one.

"Bitch, get the fuck up!" Rachael yelled.

Corrine did what she was told, quickly getting on her knees to stand up. Before she had a chance to rise completely, Rachael kicked her in her chest, knocking the wind out of her.

Falling to the floor, she grabbed her chest, gasping for breath. It felt like her chest had caved in. Rachael continued to kick, claw, and punch at her mercilessly, yelling obscenities at her.

God, please just kill me now, Corrine thought, slipping out of consciousness.

"Yeah, bitch, that's what you get! Stay the fuck away from my daughter!" Rachael said cruelly.

Turning around to face Mercedes, still in attack mode with her

adrenaline rushing, she threw a hard blow, connecting with the teen's face.

Mercedes collapsed to the ground, holding her face in pain as Rachael continued to beat on her. She wrapped her elbows around her head, trying her best to protect it.

"I hate y'all bitches!" Rachael screamed with each blow.

From the side of her eyes, Rachael glimpsed at a lamp that sat on the floor. Smiling devilishly, she ran to the lamp, lifted it, and hurled it at Mercedes, knocking the girl out. Looking at Corrine and Mercedes lying motionless on the floor, she flashed a toothless smile and left the bedroom to enjoy her next fix.

✠ ✠ ✠

It was twelve midnight when Mercedes finally awoke. Waking up in a small pool of her blood, she winced in pain as she glanced around, frantic.

The bedroom was bone-chilling cold from the winter night, causing her to shake uncontrollably. Her skin was dull and her eyes carried years of pain. She reeked of trash as she tried her best to stand to her knees, but it was to no avail. Through the dark room, she could see the silhouette of Corrine's body, still lying motionless on the floor.

Grabbing Corrine's shirt and tugging it, tears seeped down her cheeks. "Corrine, get up, girl!"

Neither word nor movement came from Corrine, sending Mercedes into a panic.

The side of her head throbbed where the lamp had hit her, and the hair there was matted in blood. Dizzy and nauseous, she walked to the closet, grabbed her duffle bag, and started to pack it with the few clothes she and Corrine owned.

She couldn't stay in that house anymore. If she or Corrine spent one more night in that house, they'd end up dead. And with that thought, she had to leave.

"God, please give us strength," she cried.

She dropped down next to Corrine, grabbing her by her hand. "Please get up; I need you!"

When Corrine's eyes finally fluttered open and she groaned, Mercedes couldn't help but flash a weak smile.

"Leave me alone, Mercedes. Face it; we're going to die here," Corrine whispered with a defeated look on her face.

"Stop talking crazy; we're getting out of here tonight, girl," Mercedes said firmly, using the little strength she had to help her up.

Wincing in pain, she finally rose to her feet. Wrapping their arms around each other's shoulders, they walked out of the room and painfully made their way to the front door. When they got to it, they stopped for a moment to rest.

"Is Tessa coming with us?" Corrine asked.

Mercedes had forgotten about Tessa. She snapped her fingers and told Corrine to stay by the door. Seeing double, she used the walls to support her as she walked toward Tessa's bedroom at the end of the hall.

When she finally walked into Tessa's room, she found Tessa on her bed, curled into a ball and crying. She continued and sat on the bed.

"Are you okay?" Mercedes whispered weakly.

Turning around to face Mercedes, Tessa smiled and threw her arms around Mercedes' neck, giving her a tight hug.

"Are y'all okay? I thought she killed y'all from the way y'all were screaming," Tessa said.

"We're good, but we're leaving for good. Are you still coming with us?"

"Hell yeah, I'm coming!" Tessa hopped out of her bed and grabbed a backpack from her closet and threw it over her shoulders.

"Aren't you going to pack some clothes in there?"

"Oh, no, they're already in there. I was already prepared for this day." Tessa shrugged.

Leaving the bedroom together, they went to the front door where Corrine was waiting for them.

Before they walked out of the door, Mercedes turned to face both girls. "Wherever we go, we have to promise each other that we'll always stick together and have each other's backs. We're sisters, and we're the only family we have right now."

"You're right, but where're we going to go?" Tessa asked. "The only place I have in mind is that woman, Sugar."

"I don't know, girl, but we're getting the hell out of here. That's all that matters," Corrine said, walking out of the door.

Both girls quickly followed behind her, never looking back.

✠ ✠ ✠

Deion sat at his kitchen table staring at the piles of *Hustling Hard* paperback and hardcover books that were scattered across it. His clothes were disheveled, his breath stank, and he was in need of a good shave. Ever since he had that talk with Day'onne and Ms. Younger, he'd moped around his condominium, lost in his thoughts.

He'd spent more than a week contemplating if he wanted to get down with Day'onne or not. Even though Day'onne was his family, and his twin brother at that, he couldn't cope with the thought of even being around him. When the three of them got separated and Deion was adopted by Ms. Younger, he'd done whatever it had taken for him to be successful.

Once he discovered at a young age that he had the gift to write, Ms. Younger, like she'd promised, had helped him hone his craft and took her time with him. She'd taught him everything she'd learned in college as an English major, teaching him the values of writing. When he'd turned twenty-one, he'd started writing *Hustling Hard.* Now that it was published, he felt as if all his hard work had paid off.

But with Day'onne popping up into his life out of nowhere telling him someone was out to kill him, he felt as if he was back at square one.

The loud ringing of his cell phone brought him back to reality.

Glancing at the caller ID, he exhaled and raised his eyebrow when a strange number popped up.

"Who is this?" he answered.

"What's up, bro? You think about what I told you?" Day'onne's deep voice boomed through the phone.

"Yeah, I did."

"Look, meet me up Northview in an hour on the corner of Penfort Street and don't be late," he said before ending the call.

Deion sighed as he stood up to finally get himself together. Walking into his spacious bathroom, he took his time shaving and bathing himself. An hour later, he stepped out of his place cleaner than he was two hours ago. Dressed in a black Gucci suit, he jumped into his BMW and made his way toward the place he hadn't seen in more than eight years.

✠ ✠ ✠

Deion cruised down Hazlet Street, bobbing his head to the loud Rakim music that blared from his radio. Looking through his tinted windows, he scanned the poverty-stricken neighbor-

hood he'd grown up in. Nickel-and-dime hustlers and other people turned, almost breaking their necks to get a peek at his car. Deion shook his head as he cruised through Penfort Street. Seeing Day'onne standing on the corner, he stepped out of the car with a grim look on his face. Day'onne, who was dressed in a blue Lacoste polo shirt, crisp black jeans, and black Polo boots, smiled as Deion walked toward him with a mean scowl on his face.

"Damn, nigga, what the fuck is wrong with you? Rolling up on me looking all mean and shit." Day'onne laughed before walking away.

Deion remained silent as he followed his brother into a nearby abandoned apartment.

Walking into the building with caution, he flinched at the sight before him. In the empty apartment, a table sat in the middle of the living room with stacks of money laid on top of it. There were a couple of people sitting around the table counting the money. In the corner, he saw a couple of drug addicts on the floor, sticking needles into their veins. When Day'onne walked him into the kitchen, Deion almost fainted because he'd never seen so many guns and drugs in his life. There in the kitchen, more than a dozen hustlers sat at two different tables with AK-47's, shotguns, .45 calibers, and .9mm's in their hands. On a different table, beautiful naked women with stacked, curvaceous physiques and surgical masks adorning their faces, cut, cooked, and bagged dope.

"What's up, Deion?" a dark, black-blue man with pearly white teeth asked.

"Who are you?"

"Awe, nigga, don't act like you don't recognize me. It's me, Menace."

"Oh, what's up?" Deion said.

Menace waved Deion off, then turned and started handing out bags of dope to his workers for them to sell. Around the time Melissa was slain, Day'onne and Menace had taken the money and drugs they'd robbed from Jewels and created their drug empire from the ground up. Starting off working themselves, they'd quickly expanded their team, having over twenty workers working for them by the time they hit nineteen. At age twenty-one, they both had touched millions of dollars. Their names were booming everywhere throughout the streets of not only Northview, but all over Pittsburgh and even New York as well. Basically, Day'onne and Menace were untouchable.

"So, this is the shit you been doing with your life?" Deion asked as he followed Day'onne into an empty bedroom.

Taking a seat in a nearby chair, Day'onne took a blunt from behind his ear and lit it. He nodded as he took a pull from it and exhaled.

"Yeah, this shit is all I know, bro." Day'onne shrugged.

Deion silently took a seat next to his brother and shook his head in disbelief.

"What you mean? There isn't shit to living this life."

"Well, not everybody could fucking make it out the hood and write a book, Deion. This shit is my ticket and I get mad respect from niggas. Shit, I even make niggas bow down to me. I'll die doing this."

"You know, when we were living with Melissa, she only wanted the best for me, you, and Corrine. I wish she could've seen the day I graduated from high school and published this book; she would've been so happy, man. But, what would she say about you? She always worried about you when you were out here robbing people and shit. What's up with you? From what I can remember, you always been like this."

"Man, fuck all that shit. She could barely put food in our mouths and clothes on our backs. I did what I had to do, so why you sweating me? I was born this way and I'll die this way."

"Alright, man; what do you want from me, Day'onne?" Deion asked, hopping up and scowling down at him.

Day'onne inhaled the marijuana, blowing out a thick cloud of smoke, trying to collect his thoughts. As he looked into his twin brother's eyes, he couldn't help but shake his head. He couldn't believe how they were identical but acted nothing alike.

"Like I told you before, I want you on my team, Deion."

"For what? And why does that man, Jewels, want us?"

"Remember the time you walked in on me and Menace with all that money in the duffle bags?"

Sitting back down, Deion tapped his chin, thinking. "I don't recall."

"Yes, you do, man. We had those duffle bags and you asked where we got all that money from!"

"Oh, yeah, I remember that now!" Deion said, snapping his fingers. "Why? What about it?"

"Well, that was the money and drugs we confiscated from Jewels. That's why Melissa was killed, because of the money we took," Day'onne admitted.

Deion sat in deep thought as he digested what Day'onne had said. His mind raced back to the time he'd overheard Shay talking about the robbery to her best friend, Cherry, and when he'd walked in on Day'onne and Menace with the duffle bags. It all made sense. He wanted to kick himself for not realizing that earlier.

"Man, why would you do that? You had something to do with Melissa's death and you're just now telling me this?"

"I know, man. I fucked up, Deion. I'm not going to lie; I regret doing that shit, even until this day. I miss Melissa, man. But the damage is already done; we can't take it back."

"You're heartless, man. What do you want from me, Day'onne? Where do I fall in with this?"

Taking the blunt out of his mouth, Day'onne stared into his brother's eyes. "I want you to ride, Deion. We're family. Yeah, we might've never really been close, but when it comes to our lives, we got to stick together. I want to train you. Teach you how to play your part in these streets. You might be making money from that book, but the real money is in the drug game. Plus, I'm about to open a club in the next couple of months, so you know niggas is getting paid. I never really asked you for anything, but right now, we need each other more than ever. If we work together, we could make twice the money and get rid of that nigga Jewels."

Deion looked at his glassy-eyed brother, contemplating his next move. Even though he didn't want to get caught up into the street life, he remembered all the money he had seen on the table in the living room. With that image embedded in his head, he took Day'onne's deal into consideration.

"What about Corrine?" he asked, almost forgetting about her.

"What about that bitch?" Day'onne spat harshly. "We don't even know if she alive or not. This is about me and you, Deion. We all we got. Jewels probably killed her a long time ago."

With his mind flooded with memories of Corrine, Day'onne raping her, and Melissa being killed because of Day'onne, he swallowed the huge lump in his throat as he pushed them to the back of his mind and said, "I'm in."

Smiling, Day'onne shook his brother's hand and took another pull from his blunt.

CHAPTER TWELVE

"Hey, Daddy!" Jewels' five-year-old daughter, Yazmin, yelled before jumping into his lap.

"What's up, baby girl? How's daddy's little girl?" Jewels asked, flashing a bright smile as he looked into his daughter's dark, chinky eyes.

"Good! Momma said when are you going to take her shopping?"

"Tell Momma I said leave me alone," Jewels said, looking up at his baby's mother and shaking his head.

Relisha ignored him as she got up off the sofa and strutted into the kitchen. He watched her leave the living room, loving the sight of the natural bounce of her plump apple bottom. They were all posted in Jewel's condominium located on the outskirts of Pennsylvania. The place was decorated in a red and black elegant décor. The living room was furnished to perfection with black wraparound sofas and body-length mirrors decorated the walls. The floor-to-ceiling windows, stainless steel kitchen appliances, and cream-colored walls made Jewels' place warm and comfortable.

Jewels, who was dressed in a pair of baggy sweat pants and a white T-shirt, gently sat Yazmin on the couch and got up and walked into the kitchen. His once clean-shaven head was now nappy and knotted and his powerful aura had diminished.

"Why the fuck you keep asking me to take you shopping?" he asked in his low, cold voice as he walked into the kitchen.

"Because your daughter and I need some clothes. Plus, I'm tired of resting my head in Northview while you get to lay up in this nice place," Relisha fussed.

"You know my money is tight. I just got out the joint a couple of months ago; I'm trying to lay low and get my shit together."

Relisha rolled her eyes and folded her arms under her breasts.

"Fuck that, me and your daughter is tired of riding around in that lame ass Caravan while you ride in an Escalade! I'm tired of you acting like you don't have any money when you know damn well you do!"

Seeing him clench his jaw, she smiled, knowing she'd struck a nerve. Five years ago, before he'd gotten locked up, Jewels had scooped her up off the streets and gotten her into a rehab, trying to find more information on Day'onne. After getting out of rehab and going back to her old image, before the drugs, he couldn't help but take her home and sex her.

The first night they had sex, Relisha ended up getting pregnant. A couple weeks later, Jewels was in prison.

"You ungrateful bitch," he spat, grabbing her by her throat and slamming her into the wall. "You weren't complaining about money when I took your crackhead ass off those streets and got you clean! Shit, getting your ass pregnant was one thing; now you all in my spot? You better learn how to respect the hand that fucking feeds you, you ungrateful bitch!"

Relisha gasped for air as Jewels violently threw her to the ground. Tears raced down her cheek as she watched him walk out the living room and run upstairs.

Standing to her feet, Relisha ran after him.

"Where you think you going?" she asked, watching him step out of his clothes.

"Don't worry about it. Take my daughter and go home, Relisha. I got business to handle."

"Fuck you, too, motherfucker," she mumbled under her breath, walking out the room.

✠ ✠ ✠

"What's going on, man?" Jewels said as he walked into Respect's apartment.

Respect, who was seated on his sofa, hopped up and gave his best friend a hand dap. "Shit, chilling, you know? How's everything?"

"Same shit, man; just a different day. Trying get my weight back up, you know what I mean?"

"I hear that. I wake up every day thinking about what I used to have. Look at this shit," Respect said, glancing around his small place. "This is a far cry from what we used to have; by now we're supposed to be retired from the game, sitting on millions."

Five years ago, Jewels, Respect and Wise had gotten locked up and lost everything. The FBI had been seeking Jewels and his operation out for more than ten years but since Jewels was always smart and two steps ahead of everyone, they never could find anything to charge him with. But after stopping Loyal one day for a broken tail light, they'd searched his car and found over fifty grand worth of pure cocaine bricks in his car. Folding under pressure after the FBI threatened to smack him with a life sentence, Loyal snitched on his entire team. He told them everything from where all of their stash houses were located to the Cuban connections.

After finally getting an approved search warrant, the FBI had wasted no time invading all of Jewels' spots, completely wiping him out. They seized all of his bank accounts, cars, houses, and even his club before finally arresting not only him, but his whole crew and workers. Since they didn't have any evidence of any of the drugs in the stash house tracing back to Jewels, the judge

smacked him with a four- to seven-year bid after finding a gun in his club office. Locked up, he'd lost everything he owned, even his respect. And now that he was out, he wanted it all back and he'd do whatever it took to make it happen.

"Yeah, this shit is crazy. But what's up with that nigga, Wise?" Jewels asked.

"He still up there bending over for them niggas. I still can't believe that nigga gay! Wise, out of all people? That nigga used to be a straight player."

"Man, I still can't believe Loyal did this shit to us. If it weren't for him, like you said, we would've been retired by now. I'm broke as hell, that's something, I'd never thought I'd experience in my life," Jewels said, looking at the ground.

"That's why he got dealt with. But what we need to do is get back on top. Pittsburgh is still our streets! These young niggas don't know what they're doing!"

Jewels rubbed his nappy goatee before going into deep thought. His thoughts transferred to Day'onne. While he was locked up, he'd received word of how Day'onne had claimed his entire drug operation, was pushing major weight, and had Pittsburgh on lock. It made him sick to his stomach to know Day'onne had taken over his empire that he'd worked so hard to accumulate over the years. When he finally got out of prison, he had put the out on the streets that he was ready to complete the job of killing Day'onne and his family.

"I know exactly what we can do to get this money," he finally said.

"I'm listening."

"About a month ago, I put the word on the streets that I want Day'onne and the rest of his family dead. If we could get that nigga, we could get our operation back and pick up where we left off."

"Damn, you still on that shit from when he robbed you? Would you let it the fuck go? You already killed Melissa, shit!"

"Man, fuck that! I don't give a fuck if it was twenty years ago! He crossed me and he's still going to pay! Now all I want you to do is have my back, round up a few of our former workers and ride with me, man! Is that too much to ask?" Jewels barked.

"No, man, I'll do it. I'm down."

"Alright, that's all I want to hear. I can use Relisha to my advantage and she can help us get them."

"Yeah, definitely. Plus, you heard Day'onne and his right-hand are about to open a club in a couple months down in the strip district?"

"Damn, dude doing it that big?" Jewels asked enviously.

"Yep, but don't worry, we'll get him."

"Indeed."

✠ ✠ ✠

Corrine, Mercedes, and Tessa arrived at Sugar's. The three distraught, lost teenagers were dressed in filthy clothes and their hair was dirty and knotted. They stood on the front porch, nervous, contemplating their next moves.

"Are y'all sure y'all want to do this?" Tessa asked.

"What other choice do we have? It's not like we have anywhere else to go," Mercedes replied.

"Yeah, y'all are the only family I have. Like you said before, Mercedes, we're all we have and we have to stick together," Corrine said, looking at the ground.

"Who are y'all?" Sugar asked, opening her front door.

Sugar, who was a notorious pimp in Northview, stood five feet even and was a bonafide hood chick. She rocked a twenty-inch

Asian weave that touched the top of her plump apple bottom. She had smooth, dark skin and, although approaching forty, looked as if she was thirty. When she had heard faint voices on her front porch, she'd opened the door and found three young girls with duffle bags around their shoulders standing there.

"Hey, Ms. Sugar, my name is Tessa and I'm a friend of Sweety," Tessa said, referring to a former prostitute.

"Sweety? Oh, that girl made me a lot of money. I miss her; how is she doing?" Sugar asked, taking a long pull from her cigarette.

"She's good, but she told me if I ever needed a job, I could come to you?"

"How old are y'all? Y'all look awfully young."

"Fourteen, fifteen, and sixteen."

"They get younger and younger each year," Sugar whispered, shaking her head.

She had helped many young, lost females in her day. She had brought them in with open arms, teaching them how to survive in the streets while they sold their bodies to strangers.

"Okay, come in," she instructed, flicking the cigarette.

Walking into her apartment, all three girls were appalled at the sight before them.

Corrine twisted her nose up in disgust as she watched naked and half-naked women and transvestites strut around the house. Taking a seat on the sofa, all three girls tried to focus on Sugar as she began to talk.

"So, what's y'all stories?"

"What do you mean?" Mercedes asked, confused.

"Everybody that comes up in here has a sad story. Some women have kids, others are homeless, and others were runaways. Now, what's y'all stories?"

"We're homeless," Mercedes said nonchalantly.

They didn't know Sugar and they didn't want her all up in their business. They were there for only one thing and that was to make money.

"Okay, I see. But this is how it goes, I put y'all on the corners, and y'all fuck and suck as many men as you possibly can in that one night. Whatever you bring home that night, I get half of it," Sugar stated bluntly.

The girls swallowed the huge lumps in their throats as they nodded.

"Now, are y'all sure y'all are ready for this? Because I'm telling y'all now, I don't play about my money and if any of you fuck with it, that's y'all throats. This is a very dangerous game y'all are getting into, so come with caution and make sure y'all have my money. Are we clear?"

"Yes," they said in unison.

CHAPTER THIRTEEN

"Who's this nigga?" Menace's brother, Troy, asked, glancing at Deion as he walked into the empty kitchen.

"That's Deion's twin, dickhead. Remember him?" Menace asked, slapping Troy in the back of his head.

"Oh shit, I remember him. What's up, nigga?" Troy said, giving Deion a hand dap as he took a seat.

Deion, Day'onne, Troy, and Menace were all seated around a table in one of their many drug houses up Northview. In front of them were stacks of uncut cocaine and heroin bricks.

"What are those?" Deion asked, pointing at the bricks.

All three men looked at Deion as if he was stupid before bursting into hysterical laughter.

"Nigga, how are you going to write a book on hustling when you don't even know what bricks look like?" Menace laughed.

"Man, forget all of y'all! Let's get this shit over with!" Deion spat.

"Alright, Deion, these are cocaine and heroin bricks," Day'onne said, holding one in his hand. "This is how we make our money."

"I know that. I'm not stupid, man," Deion retorted, cutting his eyes at Day'onne.

"Listen. I'm going to show you how to cut, cook, and bag all of this."

"Why though? This doesn't have anything to do with handling Jewels! And don't them naked-ass females do that for you?"

"Would you shut the fuck up and listen? Yeah, I want you to help me with Jewels but I want to put you down with this shit, too. I'm telling you, bro; this shit here will make you rich by the time you twenty-five. Now, chill, sit back, and learn."

"Alright; go head, man," Deion said as he watched Day'onne take a box cutter and opened the brick.

"Before you begin to cut, taste it and make sure it's the right product. Sometimes them Cubans be trying to get over on niggas, so always taste it. All you do is take a little bit of cocaine on your pinky, run it against your gums, and if it numb up, you all good," Day'onne stressed.

Deion nodded as he watched his brother continue.

"Next, take a small shank or anything sharp and cut the chunks of cocaine into small piles."

With every move he made, Deion continued to watch closely, making mental notes of what Day'onne was teaching him.

Day'onne, Menace, and Troy spent the next couple of days training Deion on how to become a certified street hustler. Deion wasn't into the street life and it was almost like pulling teeth trying to get him to listen. But, in a matter of four weeks, all three men were confident enough that he was ready for the streets and to start making that money.

When Deion walked into their main stash house one day wearing a navy blue Puma jogging suit with the matching shoes, Day'onne couldn't help but smile.

"Damn, nigga! Look at you! Finally looking like one of us. Glad you decided to put down them business suits!" Day'onne laughed and gave his brother a hug.

"You already know, nigga!" Deion smiled.

"Alright, all you need is some good pussy, now. That's why I brought you somebody I know you'd love to fuck, then duck," Day'onne said, snapping his fingers.

Deion's heart slammed into his chest when a beautiful redbone walk out of the next room. Looking into her familiar gray eyes, Deion couldn't help but smile.

"Shay? Is that you?"

"Yes, what's up, baby?" Shay smiled before giving him a tight hug.

Dressed in a pair of skintight skinny jeans, a white baby tee, and black stilettos, she licked her lips seductively as she stared at Deion. Day'onne, who hadn't forgotten about how Deion always had a crush on Shay, knew she could be the finishing touch on turning Deion into a real street hustler.

"You want to go out to eat or something?" Deion asked.

"Man, fuck that soft shit! Take that bitch to your spot and fuck her brains out!" Day'onne said, cruelly.

Shay cut her eyes at Day'onne. She held her hand out to Deion. "Sure, I'd love to go out."

Taking her by her hand, he led her out of the stash house and they were on their way.

✠ ✠ ✠

"So what have you been up to since we graduated from high school?" Deion asked as he pulled Shay's seat out for her.

He had taken her to a fancy French restaurant on the Eastside she would enjoy. Taking a seat and picking up the menu, she said, "Um, I didn't graduate from high school."

"Oh, why didn't you?" he asked, raising his eyebrows.

"School wasn't for me. I was dealing with a lot of shit, so I said fuck it." She shrugged. "But what about you? I heard you published a book? What publisher published it?"

Deion smiled. "Yeah, I wrote a book and no one did. I self-published it."

"That's good! How much money did you make off of it? I know you're making money off that shit!" she yelled obnoxiously.

Deion cleared his throat as a few couples turned and glanced at them.

"Fuck is they looking at? They all racist and shit!" Shay said, twisting her mouth up.

After ordering their food and watching Shay devour it all as if she hadn't eaten in days, Deion was finally ready to go.

"You want me to take you home?" he asked as they hopped into his BMW.

"No, why don't you take me to your place and fuck me?" Shay purred.

"No, I'm cool. I don't do that to females; you got me mixed up with Day'onne. I'll take you home."

Gripped with embarrassment, Shay folded her arms under her breasts and remained quiet the rest of the ride home. When he arrived in front of her apartment up Northview, Deion gave her a soft kiss on her cheek and watched as she hopped out of his car in anger.

✠ ✠ ✠

"Boy, what do you have on?" Ms. Younger asked when Deion walked through her front door.

Seeing his pants sagging, exposing his Calvin Klein boxers, her pink lips dropped in shock.

"Clothes, Ma. You like it?" Deion laughed, rubbing his hands together and licking his lips.

"No, you look like one of them hood boys! Pull them pants up!" she yelled.

"Well, just because I'm not wearing a suit don't mean anything. I like wearing these; it's cool, Ma! Day'onne ha—"

"Day'onne? What about him?" she asked, cutting him off.

"I was just with him and—"

"Why were you with him? He's nothing but trouble!"

"Would you let me talk? You're the one that told me to talk to him anyways! He's cool, Ma. He was teaching me a few things."

"When I said that, I didn't mean go change yourself. Look at you, walking in here with your pants sagging! You are a gentleman; Melissa taught you better than that. And what has Day'onne taught you?"

"Damn, would you fucking chill? Like you've said before, Day'onne is my family and I have to have his back. Don't worry, Ma, I got this," Deion assured her.

"Would I 'fucking chill?' Look how you're talking to me! You have this book to worry about so watch what you get yourself into, Deion! I just want the best for you."

"Man, fuck that book! You told me that I need to be there for my family and now that I am, you talking about this book. Which one is it, man?" Deion yelled, startling Ms. Younger.

Smacking him across his face, Ms. Younger pointed her freshly manicured nails toward her front door. "Get your ass out of my house and don't come back until the Deion I truly know is back!"

Deion flared his nose in anger as he walked out her front door.

CHAPTER FOURTEEN

"Take a seat, I want to school y'all on a few things," Sugar said, pointing toward her sofa.

Corrine, Mercedes, and Tessa nodded before taking a seat and staring up at Sugar. They all appeared nervous and anxious as they waited for their lesson.

"Like before, I'm warning y'all, this business is very dangerous. Y'all will be in those streets day in and out, so y'all have to be safe," Sugar said, reaching into her purse and removing three box cutters.

She handed them to the girls before continuing.

"If y'all ever feel like y'all are in danger, all you do is flick that button on the side up, angle the blade, and slice. Keep that on y'all twenty-four-seven, understand?"

All three girls nodded as they continued to listen.

"Okay, next thing; if any of you were ever to get arrested and the police ask you who do you work for, always tell them yourselves. As a matter of fact, don't say anything. I don't want any of those nosy ass cops in my business.

"And lastly, and on this one, I want y'all to listen; if any of you see any other bitch that work here dead in them streets, leave them there. Only do something if you see them in danger; go and help them out. Don't never, I mean *never*, call the police or nothing. Tell me and I'll handle that, understand?"

Mercedes nodded nervously, finally allowing the dildo to slowly penetrate her opening. All three girls winced in pain as the fake penises entered their vaginas. The pain was excruciating. A few minutes later when their painful moans didn't subside and they were running away from the dildos, Sugar ordered for them to stop as she whispered to herself, "This is going to take longer than I thought."

✠✠✠

After teaching the girls how to sex each other on the dildos, Sugar knew they were ready. It was five in the evening, and she had three skimpy outfits stretched out on her La-Z-Boy chair, ready for them to try them on.

Tessa was dressed in a pink leather, two-piece outfit with a sleeveless top that exposed her flat stomach and B-cup breasts. The short skirt showed off her curvaceous legs.

She gave Mercedes a black, sleeveless dress, with knee-length hooker-heel boots. Her hair had been cut into a short, inverted bob that made her look much older.

Corrine, on the other hand, wore a fiery red, sleeveless dress that accentuated her light, creamy skin and round, heart-shaped bottom. Sugar had styled her hair into a Chinese blunt cut wrap that made her look older, too.

"Y'all ready, girls?" she asked, looking them up and down.

She knew all three of the girls would bring at least a grand home tonight.

"I guess…" Corrine said nervously.

She tapped her chin, then pulled out a blunt laced with cocaine and lit it.

"Y'all want to hit this blunt?" she asked.

"I'm cool. I don't smoke," Mercedes said, shaking her head.

"Chill, lil' ma. This shit here will help y'all get through this; trust me. All y'all got to do is smoke this before y'all fuck," Sugar assured them.

"What is that? That don't smell like weed," Corrine said.

"It's laced weed. All y'all got to do is smoke. Shit, I'm not trying to force y'all. I'm trying to help y'all. I know how it is the first night. Trust me, it'll be a long night if y'all sober." Sugar shrugged, taking a long pull at the blunt.

Tessa hesitated for a minute before taking the blunt out of Sugar's hand and taking a long pull on it. She choked as the vicious drug raced through her body, filling her insides up and warming them. Corrine and Mercedes followed suit, taking the blunt from her hand and taking a longer, deeper pull. The two cough violently as the drug entered their young lungs. A couple minutes later, the three girls were feeling good, maybe a little too good.

They strutted out the front door with Brainiac by their sides, ready for their first shift. When the girls got on the streets, they were feeling both nervous and good with their adrenaline rushing.

"Are y'all okay?" Brainiac asked them.

"Yeah, guess we got to do what we got to do, right?" Tessa asked, shrugging.

"Yeah, we all do, girl. It's not hard, though. When you're not sober, the time seems to go by in a blur and before you know it, it's all over and you have a wad of cash in your hand if you play your cards right."

"So it's that easy, huh?" Mercedes asked.

Her eyes appeared low and red from the laced weed she'd smoked. It felt as if she was floating in the air as she stood on the corner, waiting for her first client to approach her.

"Yes, it's that easy, but watch out for cops; they be lurking. Do y'all have y'all box cutters?"

All three girls nodded.

"Okay, watch and learn," Brainiac said, strutting off.

She walked toward a nearby car that flicked his headlights twice, signaling that he was a trick. Hopping into the passenger's side, she turned toward the girls and winked before the car drove off.

For an entire hour, all three girls stood on the corner frozen in fear.

When Brainiac came back and hopped out of the car, she shook her head in pity.

"Why are y'all still here? Sugar will really kill y'all if y'all don't hand her at least five hundred dollars tonight."

"We can't do it, Brainiac. We thought we were ready…but we can't do it," Tessa said, tears forming in her eyes.

Reaching into her bra, Brainiac shook her head and she removed a piece of foil and unfolded it.

"What are those?" Mercedes asked, looking at the small pills that were in the foil.

"Ecstasy pills. If y'all take these, y'all should feel more relaxed." Brainiac handed each girl a pill.

They popped the pill in their mouths, forcing themselves to swallow it with their saliva. A couple minutes later, they felt more relaxed and felt warm moisture in between their legs from the effect of the ecstasy. They watched as every man that rode past them honked their horns, trying to get their attention. Corrine, being the bold one, decided to get into a white, old-school Chevy that was sitting pretty on spinning rims. Tessa hopped into a baby-blue BMW and Mercedes, on the other hand, climbed into an old station wagon. All three girls decided to meet up an hour later, no earlier and no later.

Hopping into the Chevy, eyes bloodshot, Corrine immediately got to work, fumbling with the driver's zipper and pulling out his penis.

"Oh, shit," the driver mumbled, pulling into a parking lot.

She took a condom out of her bra and tried to open it with her teeth, but the man wasn't having it.

"No, Ma, I don't like condoms. I want to feel inside. Raw."

Corrine contemplated her next move.

Sugar had warned all of her girls to always wear a condom no matter what. No glove, no love. But high off the laced blunt and ecstasy, she shrugged, tossed the condom, and spread her legs.

✠ ✠ ✠

Mercedes sat in the back of the station wagon with her legs spread open, trying to hold back the tears that were threatening to come out. Even though she was high off the drugs that were given to her earlier, the pain was still excruciating. Biting her lip, she closed her eyes and imagined she was anywhere else except there, in a stranger's car, getting her back blown out. When the man finally ejaculated into the condom and fell on top of her in exhaustion, she was thankful it was over.

A couple minutes later, after the man caught his breath, he reached into his pocket and pulled out a crisp hundred-dollar bill.

He tossed it at her, saying, "Alright, hoe. Get the fuck out!"

✠ ✠ ✠

"Bend that ass over and arch your back," Tessa's client instructed her.

She did what she was told, bending over the seat and arching

her back. She winced in pain when he gripped her long hair and forced himself into her. Her legs trembled as a wave of pain and pleasure overcame her. She threw her round ass back, moaning as he hit every inch of her insides.

A couple minutes later, she had already experienced her first orgasm. When her client ejaculated into the condom and threw her a hundred-dollar bill, she hopped out of the car with a satisfied smile on her face.

✠ ✠ ✠

The next day, Corrine, Mercedes, and Tessa tumbled into Sugar's apartment, exhausted and ready to get some rest before they turned their next clients.

Sugar, who'd lain on the sofa all night, looked up at the three young girls and smiled.

"So how were your first tricks? You like it?" she asked anxiously.

"It was nothing." Corrine shrugged, pulling out a wad of cash from her bra.

All three girls had turned more than ten clients, allowing them to make over a thousand dollars their first night. Peeling off five hundred dollars, they handed Sugar the money and walked upstairs. Walking into the guest room, all three girls collapsed onto their beds in exhaustion. Corrine and Tessa quickly fell asleep while Mercedes curled into a ball and silently cried to herself.

CHAPTER FIFTEEN

THREE MONTHS LATER...

Deion strolled through the Westside, pushing his candy-green Aston Martin with his girlfriend, Shay, by his side. Deion glanced at the woman that had had his back for the past three months, licking his full, juicy lips seductively as he pulled into a nearby movie theater's parking lot.

"Baby, why you bring us here? I wanted to go shopping!" Shay pouted, curling her lips and folding her arms under her C-cups.

Deion shook his head, hopped out of his car, and walked over to the passenger's side and opened her door.

"I took your ass shopping yesterday. All I want to do is chill and lay low. See a quick movie before we head back to my spot."

"But I wanted that new Gucci bag, baby! We can see a movie tomorrow or something. Please, can we go, baby?" Shay begged.

"Damn, Shay!" Deion barked. "You'll get that shit another time! Don't I always give you what your ass fucking want? Why can't we kick it every once in a while, huh?"

Shaking his head, he started walking toward the theater's front doors. Instantly knowing she had messed up, she hopped out the car, slammed the door behind her, and ran after him. Her Jimmy Choo pumps clicked against the cement as she strutted toward him, intent on fixing her mistake.

"Wait, baby, damn!" she yelled, grabbing Deion by his strong, muscular arms.

"What do you want, Shay? Take the fucking car and go shopping like your ass wanted to. I'm gon' see the movie with or without you."

Shay discreetly grabbed his thick member, rubbing it through his jeans. She smiled mischievously as she felt his penis become rock-hard.

"Ahh, c'mon, baby. Don't be mad at me. I was playing. Why don't we still go see that Eddie Murphy movie like we planned?" she said, continuing to rub him.

Deion sighed deeply before grabbing her by her hand and walking toward the ticket booth. After paying for their tickets, the couple walked side by side, smiling, appearing to be the perfect epitome of love.

In the three months he'd been involved with Shay, he'd grown to love and cherish her, but he couldn't help but think that she didn't feel the same. His instincts were telling him she was a gold-digger, while his heart was telling him different. He wanted to believe that this woman loved and cared for him. A tear ran down his cheek, surprising him. He quickly wiped his face and toughed up.

"You okay, baby?" Shay asked, tugging at his shirt.

"Yeah, why you ask that?"

"No reason. You seem tense."

"I am a little."

She smiled and glanced around the theater, checking to make sure no one was aware of what she was about to do. Since they were at the very top row and it was dark, she knew she was all good. Without warning, she unzipped his pants, her eyes bucking and her mouth watering as she whipped his enlarged penis out and held it in her hand like it was gold. Deion kept quiet as he watched her wrap her juicy lips around his penis and flicked

her tongue up and down his shaft. Throwing his head back in ecstasy, he groaned, enjoying the pleasurable ride.

✠✠✠

When they arrived home from the movies, Shay wasted no time finishing what she'd started. She let out soft moans as Deion's long, thick tongue moved up and down her neck, chin, and ears. When they got into his bedroom, he laid her onto his bed and gently parted her legs. His tongue made love to every part of her body, causing her to shiver. When he finally reached her love canal, she tossed her head back and moaned as his tongue expertly glided in and out of her.

"Please, daddy, put it in," she said as she arched her back.

Submitting to her command, he pulled down his Calvin Klein boxers and teased the opening of her vagina with the head of his penis. He slowly made his way inside her, twirling his hips in small circles as he held her tightly. He sexed her using long, hard strokes, and reaching deeper inside of her with each thrust until she felt it in her gut.

A couple minutes later, he felt he was about to ejaculate. Since he didn't have a condom on, he moved to pull out. Shay wrapped her long legs around his waist, preventing him from doing so.

When he exploded, she smiled. *Got him*, she thought as he collapsed on top of her, his chest heaving.

Deion shook his head in disgust when he finally caught his breath. "What the fuck was that about, Shay?"

"What you talking about, baby?" she asked, feigning ignorance.

"You fucking leg-locked me! Stop acting stupid! Are you trying to trap me? What you trying to do? Get pregnant?" he yelled angrily.

"I don't know what you're talking about."

Deion glared at her. Standing, he gathered her clothes and tossed them out of his room.

"Bitch, get the fuck out my fucking crib, Shay! You trifling heifer! I should've known you were nothing but a fucking skeezer!"

Stunned and at a loss for words, she quickly grabbed her clothes and stepped into them. For the whole time she'd known Deion, he'd never called her out of her name. In fact, she'd never seen him that angry.

Deciding not to add more fuel to the fire, she grabbed her Dolce & Gabbana bag and hauled ass.

✠ ✠ ✠

Relisha's chest heaved in and out as she moved her sweated-out hair out of her face. She smiled brightly after enjoying an entire hour of sex with Jewels.

"Baby, I want to ask you something."

"What's up?"

"You down for me, right?" he asked seriously.

"You already know, what is it?"

"I want you to help me with something. It'll put me back on top and you'll get everything you've always wanted."

"Jewels, you're still not telling me what it is?"

Sighing, he bit his lip. "It's Deion and Day'onne."

There was a brief pause as Relisha lay there and digested the names. Realizing it was her twin sons, she said, "So, you want me to help you set up my own kids?"

"Yeah, are you going to do it?"

Turning to face Jewels, she shook her head. "I can't, baby. Those are my kids! Why would I do that?"

"What you mean, those are your kids? When did they become your kids? That bitch, Melissa, raised them!"

Seeing the hurt in her eyes, he immediately regretted saying it. He had hit a nerve.

"Fuck that! I don't give a fuck who raised them, they're still my kids! I'm not helping you with anything!" Relisha yelled, throwing the sheets off of her naked body.

"I'm sorry, baby. I didn't mean it like that. Listen to me," Jewels said, grabbing her arm.

Sitting up in the bed, she folded her arms under her breasts and rolled her eyes. Even though she didn't know her other three kids, she still cared for them. When she'd gotten out of rehab, she wanted to search for her children and reunited with them but she didn't have the strength. In her head, it was a little too late to reunite with children that were grown already.

"You're always complaining about me not giving you anything or buying you anything, right?"

"Yeah, and?"

"Well, if you help me do this, we'll be all good. I'll be back on my shit, and you'll have anything you want, Ma. That Mercedes-Benz you always wanted, closet decked out in expensive designer gear, and even a new crib," Jewels said, throwing game at her.

She nodded and smiled at the thought of finally having everything she wanted.

"So what do you say?"

"I'm in. What do you want me to do?" she asked.

Rubbing his goatee, he said, "Day'onne will be having a grand opening for his club soon. Only major heads in the game and celebrities are invited, but I'm going to find a way for you to get up in there."

"So where do I fall in at?"

"Would you shut the fuck up and listen, Relisha?" Relisha nodded as he continued. "When you get up in there, all I want you to do is find a way to divert the twins' and their crew's attention to you. If you have to walk up in there butt ass naked and shake your ass, that's what I want you to do."

"Wait, hold up for a second," Relisha fussed, shaking her head and standing to her feet. "That doesn't make sense. Where do you fall in during all of this?"

"Don't worry about that, ma. I got this; just play your part."

"No, I want to fucking know! Where do you play in with all of this, Jewels? You asking me for a big favor and I deserve an explanation at least!"

"I said, don't worry about it. Now lay back down because it's time for round two." Jewels smiled.

"Don't your ass need to take that Viagra?" she mumbled to herself, lying back down.

CHAPTER SIXTEEN

"Would you slow down on that shit?" Mercedes asked Corrine.

Corrine ignored her as she took a couple of pinches of cocaine from a nickel bag and placed it into the blunt. Mercedes shook her head, watching her roll the blunt like a professional.

"Why don't you shut the fuck up and let me do me? I'm grown, I know what the fuck I'm doing!" Corrine snapped.

"Yeah, Mercedes, chill; we know what we doing. We can handle ourselves," Tessa said, taking the blunt out of Corrine's hands and taking a long pull from it.

Mercedes threw her hands up in surrender and walked into the bathroom to get dressed for her shift on the corner. After prostituting for three months, it still made her sick to her stomach. Sleeping with a new man every hour still gave her the same degrading feeling since she'd turned her first client.

She looked at herself in the mirror, noticing the bags that were forming under her young eyes. Sorrowful tears slid down her right cheek as she started to dress in her skimpy, midnight blue dress.

She put piles of silver eye shadow, mascara, and eyeliner around her eyes, to conceal her pain. Strutting out of the apartment in a pair of five-inch heels, she tried her best to walk with her head held high. She sashayed to the corner of Penfort Street to wait for her next client.

"What's up, ma? You looking good!" an old man said as he walked past her.

When an hour had passed and not one car had stopped for her, she was about to give up for the night. As soon as she started to walk off, a black-on-black BMW rode up by her, flashing his headlights twice. Putting on a fake smile and strutting to the passenger's side, she hopped into the seat and was at a loss for words as she locked eyes with the driver. His smooth, mocha skin, light, slanted eyes, and bald head instantly reminded her of Boris Kodjoe. She had to momentarily turn her head away from him so she wouldn't get lost in his piercing eyes.

Mustering up the strength to speak, she gave another fake smile. "What do you want today, daddy? Some bomb-ass head or the whole package?"

"Um…I never did this before. Do I take you to my place or do we do it in here?" he asked as he drove out of Northview.

"It doesn't matter."

She remained quiet the entire ride until they arrived at his place on the outskirts of Pennsylvania. Her mouth dropped open when she saw the mansion he pulled up in front of. Never in her young sixteen years had she ever seen a house as big as the one before her.

"Do you like it?" He smiled as they walked through his front door.

"Yeah, what do you do for a living? This place is gorgeous!" Mercedes laughed.

"A couple of things, but my twin got this for me. By the way, my name is Deion," Deion said, holding his hand out to her.

"I'm Mercedes," she said.

She fell in love with the cream and brown décor that decorated the mansion, giving guests a warm, mellow mood as soon as they walked in. She was immediately drawn in by the beautiful classic art designs that decorated the walls.

"Wow, this is really nice. Who decorated this place?" she asked in awe.

"I did. But would you like a glass of water or something?" Deion asked, taking off his coat.

"No, I want to honestly get down to business, so I can be on my way."

"I don't want to have sex, though."

"Then what you come here for? Time is money, baby." She scowled.

"I don't know, to talk? Have a good conversation? It doesn't matter to me."

"This isn't an escort service." She laughed, taking a seat on the brown and cream sofa.

"I know, but I'll pay you whatever you want when we're done," Deion said, walking into the kitchen.

When he returned, he had two glasses of ice cold water in his hand. He handed one to Mercedes.

"Thank you, but what do you want to converse about? You don't know me, I don't know you, so what's up?"

"I know it may be weird for you, but I really am in need of some company. Shit, I'm desperate for it, as you can see." He laughed.

"I guess, so, but, um, what's on your mind? You seem like a nice man; why are you with me and not your girlfriend?"

"My girlfriend turned out to be a gold-digger. Straight scandalous. I can't trust y'all females for shit," he spat.

"What do you mean, she was scandalous? What did she do?"

"She just was, but I don't want to talk about it."

There was a slight pause and Mercedes fumbled with her fingers and stared up at the ceiling.

"So, what about you? Why do you prostitute?" he finally asked.

"Ehh, it's the long story of my life."

"C'mon," Deion said, grabbing her hand. "You can tell me."

Where do I know him from? she thought.

"Okay, I ran away from foster home and ended up doing this."

"And?"

"What do you mean, 'and?'"

"There's always a way so why prostitute? I mean, I'm not trying to knock your hustle or anything, but you're too beautiful. I'm sure whatever you've been through you could've found a different way to make it. Prostituting isn't going to fix your problems."

Bursting out into a loud, mocking laugh, Mercedes couldn't help but shake her head.

"Wow, and this is coming from someone that doesn't know me? You don't know shit, okay? Just like I don't know you, you don't know my struggles or pain, so you can't feel my hustle."

He nodded in agreement and sat there in silence. Taking the water from off the living room table and taking a few sips from it, Mercedes got a quick glimpse of a nearby photo, causing her to spit out the water.

"Girl, what the hell is wrong with you?"

Ignoring Deion, she stood up and walked over to the photo. Picking it up, her mouth fell open and she looked from the photo to Deion.

"What is it?" Deion asked, walking up behind her.

"Who's this girl?" Mercedes asked, tears forming in her eyes.

"That's my little sister, Corrine."

Clutching the frame in her hands, she collapsed back onto the sofa, a waterfall of tears cascading down her cheeks as she looked at Corrine who appeared no older than seven in the picture. Two young boys and an older woman were in the picture with her. At first glance, Corrine appeared to be happy but when she looked closer, Mercedes could see the great pain in her eyes.

"What's wrong? Do you know her or something?" Deion asked, confused.

"Yeah, she's like my little sister. No wonder you looked so familiar!" Mercedes cried. Gazing up at him, she squinted her eyes and wrinkled up her nose. "So you were the one who raped her?"

"No! No! That was my twin brother, Day'onne. I would have never done that to her," he assured her. "So where is she now?"

"She's…prostituting…like me," Mercedes said hesitantly.

Clenching his jaw and balling up his hands into tight fists, he tried to hold in his tears. Even though he hadn't seen his younger sister in years, he still couldn't picture her selling her young body.

"Um, are you ready to go? I forgot I got to handle something," he lied, standing to his feet.

"Do you want to see Corrine?"

"Look, I said I got something to handle. Take this and find your way home," he said, handing her five hundred dollars.

"But…"

"Please, go," he said, walking her toward the door. He opened it up, pushed her outside, and slammed it in her face.

✠ ✠ ✠

Corrine sat on all fours in an abandoned building, giving oral sex to an around-the-way hustler. She stopped sucking for a moment, letting him place a trail of coke on his penis, then sniffed the whole trail up her nose. She was high out of her mind, now a full-blown addict.

The hustler smiled, using his cell phone to videotape her sucking his penis. In the three months since she had turned her first client and smoked the laced blunt, she'd gotten hooked on both.

The hustler threw his head back, enjoying every lick and suck

Corrine's slim, warm tongue threw at him. Within a couple of minutes, she had him ejaculating into her mouth and talking in tongues. She finally rose, wiping her mouth and nose.

The hustler turned his nose up in disgust, tossed a bill at her, and watched her snatch it up.

"You fucking crack-whore!" he spat coldly, flipping his cell phone closed and walking out of the apartment.

A couple hours later when her high started to wear off, she left the abandoned building, ready for her next dose. She walked through the streets of Northview with her head down, rubbing her ashy arms and scratching her pale neck.

She took the twenty-dollar bill she'd made earlier and looked around for any local drug dealer to supply her with her next fix. When she reached the top of Chicago Street, she saw a couple of them on the blocks, laughing and joking around. Walking up to them, she startled one of the dudes that went by the name of Loco. Loco quickly pulled out his pistol, aiming it at her head, causing her to urinate on herself out of fear.

"It's me!" she yelled, holding her arms up in surrender.

Loco shook his head, and then placed his gun back into his hoodie before reaching into his pockets. He pulled out a dime bag, tossing it to Corrine. Catching it, she put the money in his hand and ran to a nearby crack house, her mouth watering and body yearning for the addictive drug.

That crackhouse was the place where all the junkies went to get their fixes and go into a peaceful nod. When she walked in, she gripped the drug in her hands, shielding it with her life. Everyone up in there was known for trying to stick up the other fiends for their drugs, but she wasn't having it. Walking to a nearby corner, she picked up a dirty needle that almost every junkie had used once upon a time.

Picking up a dirty bent spoon from the ground and taking a

lighter out of her pocket, she poured some of the drug onto the spoon, lit it, and watched it melt.

When the cocaine was fully melted, she took the needle and sucked the drug into it. She tapped her arm, repeatedly, trying to find a vein.

After a couple minutes passed and still no vein formed, she pulled down her pants and underwear, spread her legs, and ejected the drug into her vagina. Her body stiffened for a second before she went into a nod, temporarily forgetting about all her pain and problems, escaping her harsh realities in this cold, dirty world.

✠ ✠ ✠

It was two in the morning when Mercedes finally arrived back into Sugar's apartment. She'd spent half of the money that Deion had given her, so she could get back home. She gave Sugar the other half of the money and asked, "Did you see Corrine?"

"Shit, I haven't seen her all day. That little girl really needs to slow down. She be disappearing for days, then coming back high. She better get her shit together soon or she's out of here," Sugar stated firmly.

Mercedes nodded and swallowed the huge lump in her throat. Running upstairs into the guest room, she found Tessa sleeping.

Turning on the lights, she walked to Tessa's bed and collapsed next to her.

"Wake up, Tessa!" she said, shaking her frantically.

"What, Mercedes? What's wrong?" she asked, sitting up and glancing around the room.

Her eyes were glassy and her hair was a tangled mess. There was dried-up cocaine caked around her nose and Mercedes noticed that she'd lost a couple of pounds.

"Remember that dude, Deion, Corrine used to tell us about?"

"Yeah, her brother?" Tessa asked, removing a small, folded up piece of foil from her bra.

Mercedes watched as she unfolded it and held it to her nose, sniffing the white powder as if her life depended on it.

"You and Corrine's asses need to slow down on that shit! Give me it!" Mercedes yelled, snatching the foil out of Tessa's hand and throwing it to the other side of the room.

Tessa jumped to her feet, running to retrieve the foil; sniffing the rest of it, she collapsed to the floor, going into a head nod. Mercedes watched in pain as slobber seeped from the corner of her younger sister's mouth. Squatting next to her, she wrapped Tessa's limp arms around her neck and helped her to her feet. She laid her in the bed, then lay next to her, stroking her hair and crying.

The next morning, she woke up to Corrine walking in the room. She barely recognized her with her pale skin, dry hair and the almost lifeless look in her eyes.

"Where were you yesterday?" she asked groggily.

"Why the fuck you worried about it, Mercedes? I was out, damn," Corrine said.

"Okay, calm down, girl. But I have some good news, Corrine. Guess what?" Mercedes smiled.

"What now?"

Taking a deep breath, she picked up Corrine's hands and and held them in her own. Corrine had been waiting for this moment for the past eight years and now that it had come, her sister would finally be happy.

"Corrine, I found your brother," she said, flashing her a bright smile.

Shrugging, Corrine stared at Mercedes. "Oh, is that all?"

"What do you mean, is that all? I thought you'd be happy."

"Fuck would I be happy for? I don't give a fuck about them! I got my own life like they got their own lives; fuck that shit!"

"Calm down, Corrine. You're speaking out of anger but—"

"I'm not speaking out of anger! I don't give a fuck about them so leave it at that, Mercedes. Now leave me the fuck alone; I need some sleep," Corrine spat venomously, climbing under the covers.

"Well, I tried," she mumbled, throwing her hands up in surrender.

CHAPTER SEVENTEEN

"You ready for the grand opening of the club tonight?" Day'onne asked Deion as they cruised through downtown in Day'onne's canary yellow Range Rover.

They'd just come from meeting with the Cubans to re-up on the drug supplies and Deion was exhausted.

"Damn, I forgot all about that damn club. What is it called?"

"Club Majestic, nigga. Are you coming?"

"Yeah, I guess so. What are you wearing?"

"I don't even know yet, but whatever you wear, make sure you look official, homie," Day'onne said. "You're representing us; every big street nigga is going to be there."

He had spent the last couple of months preparing for his grand opening and the day had finally come. He made sure only celebrities and the hustlers that rang bells in the streets were only invited to this particular event. He wanted to make sure everything was on point because his reputation was on the line.

"You don't have to remind me, Day'onne. I got this, man."

Deion remained quiet the whole way home. Ever since he'd met up with Mercedes and found out Corrine was prostituting, he couldn't help but feel guilty. He wasn't in a mood for anything except to go home and get some rest.

Day'onne pulled up in front of Deion's condominiums. "Please, Deion, whatever you do, look your best. I never really ask you for

shit, but this event is big. All the major heads in the game will be there. Look your best!"

"Alright, damn, man!"

"Alright, see you tonight at the club," Day'onne said before pulling off.

✠✠✠

"You ready for this shit to pop off tonight?" Jewels asked Relisha when she walked into his bedroom.

Knowing she had to look her best, she'd just come from shopping. Walking into Jewels' room with a Fendi bag in her hand, she smiled brightly as she pulled a brown dress out and held it against her thick frame. The dress was long-sleeved and cut out in the back with a deep plunge in the front that would turn heads.

"Damn, I'm going to get a couple numbers tonight!" she mumbled under her breath, examining herself in the mirror.

"Are you fucking listening to me? Are you ready for tonight, Relisha?" Jewels growled, grabbing her arm.

"Yeah, nigga! You asked me that like five times already!"

"I want to make sure you ready; that's it. This shit is all on you, Ma. Don't fuck it up!"

"All you want me to do is get them into one room? What could be so damn hard about that, Jewels?"

"That's not the point. When I get them niggas, I want to make sure they don't see it coming, Ma. It's your job to make sure all attention is diverted on you with that mean-ass dress. That's all you got to do, look sexy, and play your part," Jewels stressed.

"Okay, I got you, Daddy; don't worry about it."

"Alright, Ma. Just checking."

✠ ✠ ✠

When Deion pulled up in front of Club Majestic, his jaw almost dropped when he saw the large crowd of people. The parking lot almost looked like a car show with luxurious cars from chromed out Phantoms, to bright Range Rovers sitting on large rims. There was a long line of people wrapped around the building, hoping and praying to get into one of the hottest parties and grand openings of the year.

Deion took a blunt out of his pocket and lit it, taking a long, deep pull from it. He would need something to get him through the long night and marijuana would do the job. He coughed uncontrollably as he inhaled it deeply. Grabbing his chest, he exhaled, trying to catch his breath. When he finally caught his breath he rolled his shoulders back, glanced at himself in the mirror, opened up the door to his car, and stepped out.

Deion was dressed in a brown Armani suit and cream Stacy Adams gator shoes. He'd allowed his once clean-shaven hair to grow and it was now cut into a sleek temple fade. A pair of fourteen carat diamond-studded earrings adorned his ears, and a gold-diamond necklace with a Jesus charm piece hung from his neck.

Walking in front of the club, Deion met up with Day'onne, Menace, Troy, and the rest of their entourage, who'd hopped out of a black Hummer limousine.

Day'onne was dressed in a gray Versace suit with silver cuff links and a pair of black gators. He had cut his dreads into a temple fade, too.

All of the men walked with curvy, beautiful women by their sides. Day'onne walked into his club with a rare smile on his face. The crowd went crazy when they saw the twins walking side by side.

"This is the fucking life, man," Day'onne whispered to Deion as they entered.

He had hired a mass of big, beastly club bouncers to keep everything in order and on track. The club was filled to capacity with drug kingpins, family, friends, and strippers.

Deion was in awe as he walked into Club Majestic for the very first time. With the theme of money in mind, the spacious club had been decked out with green sofas, a green bar, and a green stage with a platinum pole for the strippers to work their magic. The strippers, who were all of different ethnicity, color, shape, and size, walked around the club wearing nothing but real money glued to their nipples and vaginas.

The club had three different levels. On the first floor, there was a main stage with a pole, for the strippers, a bar, and a dance floor. One the second floor, there was a velvet rope located at the top of the stairs for the VIP section, where the elite were only invited. And on the third floor, there were private rooms for the strippers and for clients who wanted to pay extra money to have personal services provided for them.

"Damn, nigga, I didn't know you were doing it like this!" Deion laughed, giving his brother a hand dap and a brief hug.

"Yeah, I told you it was going to be official!" Day'onne yelled over the loud music.

"Yo, is that Jay-Z?"

"Yeah, Jay's my nigga, but play it cool. Don't be acting like these groupies; act like he one of your niggas from the hood."

Deion nodded and he walked toward the bar. Ordering a bottle of water, Deion bobbed his head to the music as he took in the atmosphere.

"Wow, this is the life."

"Hey, big daddy!" a soft voice whispered in his ear.

Turning around, Deion's mood instantly changed as he locked eyes with Shay's.

"What do you want, man?" he asked.

Ever since the day she had tried to trap him by getting pregnant, he'd tried his best to avoid her by any means necessary. He wanted to kick himself every time he thought of the situation, knowing she was as scandalous as they come.

"I want you, daddy," she purred, seductively.

Shay was scantily dressed in a burgundy sleeveless dress that accentuated her light skin. Her natural ringlet curls were pinned to the top of her head, complementing her exotic features.

"My name is Deion and I'm not your fucking daddy, Shay. I don't want shit to do with you! Beat it!" Deion spat, gritting his teeth.

"Well, you sure don't have to be my daddy, but guess who's going to be a daddy?" Shay said, rubbing her small stomach.

At that moment, he wanted to hop out of his seat and slap the mess out of her but, being the real man he was, he kept his composure. "Look, woman, you're nothing but a foul, shady bitch that's good for nothing except laying on your back and opening up your legs. If that's my seed, I'll definitely take care of mine, but I don't want shit to do with you!"

"You don't mean that; you know you love me, baby!" Shay laughed, grabbing Deion's arm.

Deion snatched it away from her and aggressively grabbed her wrist. "Stay the fuck away from me, Shay. I've never hit a female in my life but I definitely wouldn't think twice about knocking the shit out of you!"

"You wouldn't dare!" Shay said, jumping in his face.

Flaring his nose in anger, he determined that the best thing to do would be to walk away before he did something he'd regret later.

Two hours later, when the club was completely filled to capacity

and mostly everyone had arrived to celebrate with Day'onne, Deion made his way toward the VIP section of the club where Day'onne and the rest of their crew were.

"Nigga, where the hell were you?" Menace asked Deion when he walked into the room.

Looking around the room, Deion had to do a double take at the sight before him.

In one corner, butt naked women were either giving oral sex or on their backs, having sex with the major heads or celebrities. On the other side of the room sat a small crowd of men who circled around a stripper that had round assets. They all watched in almost a trance as she shook and gyrated her body as if her life depended on it.

"I was chilling; what the fuck is going on in here?" Deion asked, twisting his nose up in disgust.

"Man, you know this is how we do it!" Day'onne slurred drunkenly, a bottle of Ciroc in his hand. He wrapped an arm around Deion's neck. "You better grab you a fine bitch up in here and get your freak on."

Feeling exhausted and tired of the racy atmosphere, Deion was finally ready to call it a night.

"Alright, man. I'm out of here."

"Damn! It's only two in the morning; the party is just starting!"

"I'm tired, but again, congrats on the club and hit me up tomorrow," Deion said, giving his brother another hug and leaving.

✠✠✠

"Isn't that one of the twins?" Respect asked Jewels.

They were seated in Jewels' old black Escalade in the parking lot of the club.

It was approaching two-thirty in the morning and it was completely dark outside. In the two cars beside Jewels sat his former worker, Cash, and ten other people who were still down for him to make a move.

"That might be Deion," Relisha said, staring at her grown son.

She fought back the tears threatening to pour from her eyes. She watched Deion through Jewels' tinted windows as he got into his car and started it, noting how many handsome features he'd inherited from her.

Wow, that's my son! she thought to herself.

At that moment, she wanted to hop out of the car and forget all about the devious plan. She wanted to run into her son's arms and apologize for all of the pain and misery she'd caused in his life. She also wanted to apologize for never being a mother. But she couldn't. Sucking up the emotions, she pushed him to the back of her mind and focused on the task at hand. It was a little too late to be interrupting his life.

"Damn, we could've got that young nigga!" Jewels yelled, clenching his jaw.

"Man, we can catch him a little later; that would've fucked up our plan. We need to worry about that nigga, Day'onne, and his right hand, Menace. They the real niggas that's pulling in dough," Respect told him.

"Relisha, are you ready?" Jewels asked, turning around to face her in the back seat.

"Yeah, I'm ready."

"Remember, make sure all eyes are on you. You used to strip at my club back in the day, so you should be used to it. Get naked and buck wild if you have to!"

Relisha nodded and hopped out of the back seat, sighing deeply. Closing her eyes, she took a deep breath, gathering herself. Open-

ing them, she held her head high and sashayed toward Club Majestic's front door.

Appearing fierce in her brown Fendi dress that complimented her smooth mocha skin, she tried to walk past one of the bouncers guarding the front door, Beast.

"Excuse me, woman. Where do you think you're going?" Beast asked, licking his black lips, checking out her thick frame.

"I'm going into the party. Is there a problem?"

"Woman, do you know what time it is? The party is over in an hour or two. Why are you so late?"

"I'm Day'onne's mother and I had to do something for my little boy," she lied.

Acting as if she'd dropped something, she bent over, exposing her neatly-trimmed vagina.

Beast almost hopped out of his suit as he watched her stand back up.

"How about we leave this party, and have a party of our own?" she asked seductively.

Beast rubbed his hands together, looking around the dark parking lot and into the club. Seeing the coast was clear, he grabbed Relisha's hand and made his way toward his car.

Sliding her hand into her pocketbook and removing her .45 caliber, she held the gun to his leg and pulled the trigger.

"Ahhh! What the fuck is wrong with you, bitch?" Beast yelled, clutching his leg that was now bleeding profusely.

She ignored him, aimed the weapon at his forehead, pulled the trigger, and walked away. Entering the club, she paused, awestruck by the lavish décor and the see-through ceilings, allowing her to see up the second floor. When she got upstairs to the VIP section, no one was guarding the velvet rope in the front door. When she walked through it, her breath got caught in her throat when she saw all eyes were fixated on her.

"Damn, who's that? That bitch is fine!" Day'onne yelled in a drunken slur as he staggered toward Relisha.

Tears formed into Relisha's eyes as she looked at him, but she kept her composure. Wrapping his arms around her, he started to feel on her breasts, making her feel uncomfortable.

"What's good, *Ma*? Are you trying to have a little fun tonight?" Day'onne whispered into her ear.

"What type of fun, baby?"

"Mmm, me and my niggas got the hotel. Swing through and we'll show you."

"No, baby, I got a better idea," Relisha purred, unwrapping his arms from around her neck.

She walked into the middle of the room, holding her arms up into the air.

"Alright, everyone, can I have your attention?" she asked.

Not hearing her, they continued to drink, smoke, and enjoy the party.

"I said can I have your fucking attention!"

The whole room quickly diverted their attention on her. She smiled and began to slowly undress. The hustlers and celebrities mouths dropped open in shock as they eye-raped each curve on her full-figured body. When Ice Cube's "You Can Do It" blared through the speakers, she arched her back, exposing her back dimples, and shook her ample ass wildly. The crowd in the room went crazy, erupting into a thunderous roar and throwing cash at Relisha, egging her on like the good old days. The other strippers watched in envy as she worked her body like the true professional she was.

As she continued to dance, without warning, a group of men charged into the room with shotguns, .45 handguns, and AK-47's in their hands. Day'onne and the rest of his crew didn't have a chance to digest what was happening until they noticed Relisha

had stopped dancing and turned toward the group of men with the guns. Diving to the floor, she wrapped her arms around her head as the whole room erupted into deafening gunfire, catching everyone off guard. Jewels aimed his gun at her, pulled the trigger, and killed her instantly.

People were dropping like flies as they tried to reach into their waistbands to remove their guns, but it was too late.

The perpetrators robbed everyone for their jewelry, money, and even drugs as they continued to shoot.

Day'onne's eyes bucked in fear as he locked them on Jewels, who held a .9mm aimed directly at him. He pulled his gun out of his waistband and quickly pulled the trigger.

Missing Jewels by an inch, he watched as Jewels pulled the trigger on his gun, but missed him, too.

Thinking quickly, Day'onne turned around and shot at the window, completely shattering it before hopping out of it.

"C'mon, man!" Menace yelled. He grabbed Troy by his shirt collar and followed Day'onne.

All three men grunted in pain when they hit the ground outside of the club. They closed their eyes tightly and winced as they tried to stand to their feet, but it was to no avail; their knees and arms wobbled, causing them to fall back to the ground. Small pieces of glass penetrated their skin as they stared up at the large crowd that was making their way out of the club. Finally standing to their feet, all three men limped their way into the crowd, blending in with it until they were in front of their car.

"I'm hit man!" Troy yelled as Menace helped him into the back seat of Day'onne's car.

"Where? You cool, man?" Menace asked his younger brother, worried.

"In my leg. I think it just grazed it. I'll be cool."

Day'onne let out a loud, angry scream as he pulled out of the parking lot and drove toward one of his safe houses.

Menace, who remained quiet, shook his head in disbelief as he digested the events that had just taken place.

"What the fuck was that shit? How the fuck did that happen when I got all those fucking bouncers in that bitch?" Day'onne growled angrily.

"Was it that nigga, Jewels?" Menace retorted. "I been told you we was supposed to handle that fool and look what the fuck that happened? On the night of the grand opening. This shit isn't good, man."

"Man, fuck all that shit! That nigga is going to get his! My word is my bond. I put it on everything I love, that nigga got to go."

When they finally arrived at his safe house, all three men limped in, gripped with anger and pain. Day'onne collapsed onto the sofa and dropped his head into his hands. He bit down hard on his bottom lip, drawing blood.

"That nigga Jewels is dead, man. This was the ultimate form of disrespect. Not only was it fucking embarrassing, but also disrespectful. He got to go!" he vowed.

✠✠✠

When Deion awoke the next morning, he was immediately hit with a massive headache from the previous night's event. He sat up in his king-sized bed, holding his head and grunting. Hopping out of the bed, he started to curse as his cell phone rang until he saw it was Day'onne.

"What's up, bro?" Deion answered.

"Yo, did you hear what happened at the club last night after you left?"

"No, what happened?"

"Turn on the news, now."

Reaching for his remote, Deion flopped back down onto the bed and turned the television on. His eyes expanded in shock and he turned the volume up.

"*We're reporting live in the Strip District, on the Southside of Pittsburgh, where once again, violence has struck. Early this morning around four, a group of unidentified men barged into a new club, Club Majestic, armed with shotguns, .45 handguns, and AK-47's, a witness has told us. These unidentified men opened fire on the owner of the club, Day'onne Jenkins, and his entourage, killing over a dozen people and injuring fifteen. The horrific event occurred at the grand opening of this establishment. Mr. Jenkins has been contacted for questioning, but police are labeling it as drug-related.*

If you have any information on this massacre, please contact your local law enforcement officials."

Deion shook his head in disbelief as he turned the television back off and directed his attention back toward his cell phone.

"Who the fuck did this shit?"

"Jewels, man. That nigga going to get his, though. But lay low for the next couple days or so and keep your heat on you," Day'onne stated, firmly, before ending the call.

CHAPTER EIGHTEEN

Mercedes sat in between Sugar's thick legs as Sugar flat-ironed her long hair. She closed her eyes tightly as the hot tool ran through her hair and almost burned her scalp. They were the only two there; the other prostitutes were on the corner making that money.

"What the hell is up with Corrine?" Sugar asked, finally breaking the silence.

The mention of Corrine's name brought Mercedes to tears, but she held them back. She couldn't believe how bad the streets of Northview and the cocaine had turned Corrine and Tessa completely out. From the very beginning, all three of the girls had vowed that they'd stick together, but to Mercedes it felt as if the promise was being broken. She hated how Corrine took all the pain and frustration she had against the world and let the hard poundings of her clients' penises and the peaceful feeling that cocaine gave her, help her to escape her reality. Taking a deep breath to calm herself, she allowed her mind to drift to all the money she was making. Even though she despised the fact that she was opening her legs up and letting any man deep in, the money somewhat soothed the feeling.

The moment she'd started making money, she'd started to stack it, refusing to touch it and hoping one day to get Corrine, Tessa, and herself out of Northview and off the streets.

She had saved more than fifteen grand and counting.

"I don't know, Sugar. She's going through some things."

"Well, um, that trick about to get the boot. Corrine and Tessa," Sugar said harshly.

Mercedes tensed up and turned around to face Sugar. "What? Why?" she asked.

"Those bitches fucking with my money. They're out there smoking that glass dick and spending my half of the money on drugs and shit. They got to go; I'm sorry."

For the past couple of weeks, Corrine and Tessa would disappear for numerous days. They were out in the streets smoking Sugar's half of the money they'd earned from prostituting. She was fed up. She'd accepted the girls with open arms and could be nice at times, but when they messed with her money, that's when she had to draw the line.

"Sugar, please give them one more chance! I'm sure they just going through things!" Mercedes pleaded.

"I know you might not want your friends out on those streets, but I'm sorry, both of them got to go. They're fucking up my money; they lucky I didn't dig in their asses yet," Sugar snapped. "But I'm going to be cool about it only because I feel sorry for those little girls. All they got to do is get their shit and get the fuck out of my crib."

A couple of tears trickled down Mercedes cheeks. Standing, she said, "Well, if they go, then I go, too, Sugar."

"What? You're my number one money-maker now!"

"Oh, well. Those are my sisters and we've always vowed to stick together no matter what. Like I said, if they go, I go, too," Mercedes said firmly.

Sugar shook her head and threw her hands up in surrender. "Alright, they got less than a month to get their shit together,

Mercedes. If they don't have any of my money up front, they're out of here."

A couple of hours later, Corrine staggered into Sugar's apartment tired and high out of her mind. Mercedes, who was already dressed for her shift, fought back her tears as she looked at her. Corrine was a far cry from the person she used to be before prostituting. Her once thick frame was now very petite and she almost looked as if she was suffering from anorexia. Her long, wavy hair was now brittle dry and broken off and her frail knees buckled with every step she took.

Mercedes pulled Corrine into her arms, sobbing and the two sank to the floor.

"What are you doing to yourself, sister? Why are you doing this?" Mercedes cried.

"Please help me," Corrine said through her dry, cracked lips.

She broke down in Mercedes' arms, wailing out a low, agonizing scream. Mercedes rocked her in her arms, assuring her it would all be okay.

"I'm going to get you and Tessa some help, girl."

"Where is Tessa?"

"I don't know. Do you want me to check upstairs?"

"Yeah, can you go get her? I want to ask her something."

Mercedes nodded and unwrapped her arms from around Corrine's body.

"You stay here, I'll go see if she's upstairs."

Corrine watched through bloodshot, glassy eyes as Mercedes ran upstairs. When the sound of her sister's footsteps faded, she turned and ran out of the house, digging into her pocket, making sure her nickel bag of cocaine was still there.

Running into the usual crack house, she went into a corner and squatted, shaking uncontrollably. Repeating her normal routine,

she grabbed a dirty needle and bent spoon from the ground. When she was done preparing the drug and was ready for her injection, she heard a faint sound coming from the next room.

Slowly standing, her body trembling, she cautiously walked into the next room. Squinting, she saw a familiar emaciated, light-skinned girl sitting in a corner with her long legs pulled up against her chest and mumbling under her breath. The small girl's eyes appeared dark and empty.

"Tessa? Is that you?" Corrine cried, kneeling next to her.

"I need some, Corrine. I need it now!" Tessa mumbled in a daze.

She fell to her side and vomited, her slim hands clutching her stomach.

Corrine sighed and grabbed Tessa's arm. Amid the numerous needle track marks, she found a small vein protruding. Taking the needle that she'd already prepared for herself, she breathed deeply and slowly injected Tessa with it.

Tessa's body tensed, then went limp. Her head falling back, she went into a nod.

Tears falling, Corrine wrapped her slim arms around Tessa's frail frame."Things will get better for us, sister. Things will get better."

✠ ✠ ✠

Jewels sat in one of his old safe houses with Respect and the rest of his former workers.

All twelve men sat around a table, counting the money they'd taken during the shoot-out and robbery at Club Majestic. That night, Jewels and his team had stolen over a million dollars worth of jewelry, money, and even drugs.

"Who the fuck keeps bricks at their club? They're some of the

dumbest niggas I know," Jewels' worker, Brooke, laughed as he fingered through the money.

Jewels, who sat at the table in deep thought, couldn't fathom the thought of Day'onne still breathing. Even though Jewels, Respect, and the rest of his team had killed a dozen of Day'onne's workers, Jewels still wasn't satisfied because Day'onne was still alive.

"You good, man?" Respect asked, noticing something was bothering him.

"I still can't believe this nigga is still breathing. How the fuck did we miss? How the fuck did we let him, Menace, and Troy get away?" Jewels growled, standing to his feet and shaking his head.

"Don't stress it, boss. That nigga going to get his, believe that. Maybe not today or tomorrow, but we'll get him," Brooke said.

"No, I can't sleep with the thought of that nigga still alive. I got to get him before he gets me. I can't sleep with the thought of how many times that nigga has violated me."

"Well, at least that bitch Relisha dead." Respect shrugged.

Respect didn't have one care in the world for Day'onne. He was ready to get back on the streets and make that money once again. He was middle-aged now and it had been too long since he'd been at the top of his game. He wanted to be back up there. He craved to be.

If they took all of the money they'd stolen and flipped it, they'd be making twice as much as they'd robbed them for in no time.

"Man, fuck that bitch," Jewels said, rubbing his salt-and-pepper goatee.

As if he'd just had an epiphany, he snapped his fingers and flashed a bright smile. "Yo, don't he got a younger sister?"

"Yeah, but that bitch a crackhead hoe; the whole fucking Northview been in that." Brooke laughed.

"Yeah, I think I got her on video sucking some young nigga off," Cash said.

Jewels nodded and sat back down. He looked around the wooden table as he folded his hands behind his head. "Hmm, maybe we could get her next?"

"What? That nigga don't give a fuck about her! Day'onne's a cold motherfucker. If he cared about her, she wouldn't be out there fucking for money while that nigga sitting on millions," Brooke said.

"You right, young buck. But what about his twin? Deion?"

"That nigga be low-key. How are we going to catch him?"

"Good point. But I'm sure he be with Day'onne at times. If we get Corrine and get in contact with him for some ransom money, we could get both of them bitches."

"Sounds good. Kill two birds with one stone!" Respect laughed evilly.

"Indeed!" Jewels smiled, nodding his head and rubbing his hands together.

CHAPTER NINETEEN

"What's up, bro?" Deion asked as he hopped into Jarell's silver Benz.

"What's up? How you holding up, my brother?"

"Man, not good. I need to clear my head," Deion said, shaking his head.

He pulled out a blunt and lit it.

"Damn, when did you start smoking?" Jarell laughed.

"A couple of months ago. But, what's good with you? You good?"

"Oh, yeah, you already know. I'm glad that I decided to get out of the streets when I had a chance. It isn't the same anymore. Niggas snitching on they own people and shit? No, I had to go."

"I feel you. That's what's up, though."

"Thank you. But what about you? What's good with your book? I don't hear you mention it anymore."

"Man, I don't even know. I don't think I'm going to write again. There isn't any money in the writing industry like in these streets," Deion said, shrugging.

Jarell's Benz came to an abrupt halt, startling Deion. Jarell looked at Deion as if he'd lost his mind. "What the fuck you mean?"

"I don't know. I—"

Jarell's deep, baritone voice boomed, surprising Deion. "You what, Deion? You what? Too caught up in these fucking streets? The money?"

"I guess. But—"

"But what, man? I've never seen anyone in the fucking hood that was so career-driven like you were. You had so much potential, bro. You wrote a fucking book and you made it out of the hood! Then you came back hustling for that nigga, Day'onne? Talking about you done with writing? What the hell is wrong with you?" Jarell growled angrily.

"Man, fuck all that. Day'onne is my family and he needed me!" Deion yelled.

Sighing, Jarell pulled over to the curb and parked. Turning to Deion, he said, "Look bro, get the fuck out of these streets before it's too late. These streets don't love anyone. Not you, me, or Day'onne. The streets are talking, and they're gunning for your brother and the rest of your team."

"Who?"

"Jewels! That nigga want y'all heads on a platter. Get out of this game, Deion. I know he's your family and you want to be there for him, but sometimes you got to think about yourself. Sometimes, family isn't everything. Day'onne's nothing but a cold-hearted motherfucker that'll run over anybody to stay on top. You've got too much talent and brains to be on these streets, bro. You've got to use them," Jarell said firmly.

"How the fuck you going to tell me all of this when you always wanted me to work for you?"

"That was back in the day, Deion. Are you fucking listening? This world is cruel like your brother! Wake the fuck up! He doesn't give a fuck about you nor anyone else except himself. If you don't get out now, you'll regret it later."

Deion put his head down into his hands. "Man, I don't know, Jarell. It's like I'm already knee-deep into this shit. The money and fast life, it's addicting."

"Let me tell you this, when you were younger, everyone in the hood spoke highly of you, even the hustlers. You weren't in the streets, you graduated from high school, and then you wrote a book. Successful! How many people do you know make it to see eighteen, living in Northview, Deion? Everyone wants the best for you, bro. Like I said before, Day'onne's your twin and you want to be there for him, but sometimes you have to do what's best for you."

Deion nodded, soaking up and digesting everything Jarell was spitting to him. His friend was right.

"Speaking of family, you know your little sister out here strung out? I saw her the other day up Northview and shit. She out here selling her body and on drugs. She needs you, bro. You talking about you need to be there for Day'onne, but you need to be there for your younger sister."

Deion nodded again, holding his tears that were itching to fall. Every time he thought about Corrine, he couldn't help but feel guilty.

"Alright, bro. Thanks for the talk, I needed this. I'm going to catch up with you later," Deion said, getting out of the car.

"Alright, don't forget what I said. I really hope you take heed to my advice."

✠ ✠ ✠

An hour later, Deion arrived at Day'onne's condominium with his mind still on his conversation with Jarell.

Walking into the front door, he saw Day'onne, Menace, and Troy sitting at the dining room table with empty bottles of Vodka in front of them.

The three men looked as if they hadn't bathed in days. They

appeared rough and stressed out compared to Deion, who was clean-shaven.

Day'onne glared at Deion. "About time you got here. Where the fuck were you at?"

"I was handling some business. What's up with y'all? Why y'all look like y'all haven't washed your asses in days?"

"Man, fuck all of that, we got to worry about getting this money and that nigga Jewels."

"We were been supposed to get that nigga, Day'onne. And getting this money? We got plenty of it!" Deion gritted his teeth.

"What? Too much money ain't enough money. And when those niggas hit us at the club, they killed most of our workers and took a lot of our product. Plus, the Feds closed my club and I've been losing money by the second," Day'onne admitted.

"Losing money? What were you doing having the product up in the club? How much they rob us for?"

"They took over fifteen bricks and it's only us four. Since we don't have those young niggas on the blocks making the money for us, we got to do it ourselves," Menace said.

Deion shook his head in disbelief, taking in what he'd heard. At that point, he knew he was definitely going to take heed to Jarell's advice. He was finally tired of the streets. "Four? No, man, I'm out."

"Out? What the fuck you mean, you out?" Day'onne barked, hopping in his brother's face.

Deion tightened his jaw and clenched his fists. He knew how dangerous Day'onne was and he refused to let him get a first hit. "You heard what the fuck I said. I'm out. This shit isn't for me, yo. Y'all on y'all own."

"On our own? Oh, so when shit starts to fall down you want to bitch out like the pussy you always were?"

Without warning, Deion drew his arm back and threw a massive blow at Day'onne, connecting with his right cheek. Day'onne grunted in pain as he tumbled to the floor. Hopping back to his feet, he ice-grilled Deion and pulled his .40 caliber from his waistband, aiming it at him. Deion charged at him. Since Day'onne was drunk, he wasn't fast enough to get a hold on him. Taking the gun from him, he threw it across the room and began punching his brother. Stopping abruptly, he said, "I should beat the fuck out of you, nigga. Raising a fucking gun at me? Next time, you better pull the trigger. Like I said, I'm out the game and that's final."

"Fuck you, Deion!"

Menace and Troy watched the two brothers, clueless, not sure what to do.

They watched as Deion walked out the dining room and front door, refusing to look back.

CHAPTER TWENTY

Day'onne sat in a bar on the Westside, slowly drinking his life away. His hair was wild and untamed, his clothes were disheveled, and his face was drained. He still had a bruise and a couple of scratches on his face from the fight he'd had with Deion a couple of days earlier. People who walked past him couldn't believe their eyes. This was a far cry from the Day'onne they knew. He wouldn't dare come out of the house appearing the way he was.

"What's up, ma?" Day'onne said to the bartender, Ly'Mia.

Ly'Mia fixed her nose up in disgust and ignored him as she started to clean off the bar counter and glasses. Looking at her round assets, he licked his lips and rubbed his crotch.

"I know you hear me, bitch! I said, what's up?"

"What do you want? Don't you have a fucking bank to rob?" Ly'Mia spat cruelly.

"Bank to rob? Bitch, I got millions," Day'onne lied. "Do you know who the fuck I am?"

"Millions? You could've fooled the hell out of me with the way you look! It barely looks like you got a pot to piss in. You don't have any fucking millions, you broke as hell!"

Day'onne looked down at his clothes, then back up at Ly'Mia. Slamming his glass down, he stood up. Ly'Mia shivered and swallowed the lump in her throat. Looking into his icy, blood-red eyes, she instantly regretted what she'd said.

Day'onne wrapped his cold, beastly hands around her neck, trying his best to take the air away from her lungs. His face was the mask of a demon as he wrinkled up his nose and tightened his grip.

When a small crowd of men saw what was happening, they jumped to their feet and ran over to Day'onne, grabbing and pulling at his clothes, begging him to stop.

His chest heaving, he let her go. She collapsed to the ground, gasping for air and trembling, tears rushing down her cheek.

"Bitch, you better watch what the fuck you say to me. I will never be broke!" he spat.

Walking out of the bar, he got into his Lexus and drove off. Making his way toward Northview, he was still gripped with anger over Ly'Mia calling him broke.

I need something to take my anger out on, he thought.

When he arrived up Northview, he searched the streets looking for something to get himself into. When he saw a small, light-skinned girl posted on the corner, he drove his car up next to her and honked the horn.

Tessa folded her arms under her small breasts and wiped her runny nose. "You looking for a good time, baby?" she asked, going into a coughing fit.

Day'onne nodded as he unlocked the door, signaling for her to get into the car. When her fragile body sank into the leather seat, he pulled off. Five minutes later, he pulled in front of an abandoned apartment building and stepped out of the car. Tessa got out and followed him into a cold, empty room in the back.

Day'onne wasted no time pulling down his pants and Calvin Klein boxers and lying down on the single, dirty mattress that addicts and prostitutes used for their clients.

"Suck this dick, bitch!" he spat, gripping her hair.

She winced as he aggressively thrust his penis into her mouth,

turning it dry with every forceful pound. At that moment, she regretted even turning this client, but she was desperate for the twenty dollars that she could use to get her next fix.

Judging by the way he gripped her hair and forced his penis down her throat, she had no choice to do what she was told or else.

Grabbing the base of his penis, she teased his penis with the flat and tip of her long, slim tongue. When he eased the tight grip he had on her hair, she had him where she wanted him, so she went to work.

Day'onne stiffened and balled up his fists, trying not to moan out loud.

Before Tessa knew it, he was already ejaculating. She cringed as the salty flavor seeped down her dry throat.

"Come here," he barked, grabbing her by her throat and violently slamming her on the mattress.

Tears blinded her vision as she let out a loud, guttural scream as he forcefully parted her legs and vigorously entered her, pounding her tight, dry walls mercilessly. His grip around her neck became tighter and she gasped for air, clawing her nails into his hands, trying to get him to release her.

When Day'onne saw her eyes rolling to the back of her head and her body shaking violently, it aroused him even more, causing him to ejaculate again. He collapsed on top of her, his chest heaving. When he caught his breath, he got out of bed and got up. Seeing that her body was limp and her eyes aimlessly stared into space, he realized he'd killed her.

"Damn, what a waste of some fire pussy!" He laughed wickedly, tossing a twenty at her corpse and walking out.

✠ ✠ ✠

"Have you seen Tessa lately, Corrine?" Mercedes asked.

It was nine in the morning and the two of them lay in their dark room alone after enduring a long day and night of turning clients the previous day. Corrine lay in her bed yearning for a hit, her scary-thin frame shaking under the thin sheets. She shook her head slightly and wiped her nose with the back of her hand. It had been over a week since anyone had seen Tessa, and Mercedes was finally getting worried.

At first, she thought Tessa was ripping and running the streets, disappearing for days like she usually did. But this time, Mercedes' instincts were telling her something wasn't right. She decided to go out and find Tessa herself.

Even though she was exhausted, she got out of bed. After taking a bird bath and throwing on a pair of sweat pants and tank top, she walked downstairs and out of the door.

Walking up Penfort Street, her restless eyes took in the gloomy neighborhood. She watched hustlers hugging the corners and drug addicts yearning for their morning doses. Walking through the row houses, she looked high and low for Tessa, circling the whole neighborhood. After searching for what seemed like hours, she came up empty.

"Hey, have you seen my younger sister, Tessa?" Mercedes asked a local drug dealer. "She's light-skinned and very small?"

"Oh, you talking about that crackheaded hoe? No, I haven't seen her, but when you see her, tell her I got a free nickel bag for some free pussy." The hustler laughed.

Mercedes clenched her fists in anger and gritted her teeth. "What the fuck you just say?"

"Chill, ma, I'm fucking with you. But if I was you, I would check the abandoned houses. She usually be over there on Chicago Street."

Mercedes nodded and made her way to Chicago Street. She kept her head down, fighting tears, as she passed bystanders throwing vicious words at her, calling her a "nasty hoe."

Exhaling heavily, she looked at the dull-colored apartment buildings that had either been burned or completely abandoned. Walking into one of them, she cringed at the sight of multiple addicts in corners in head nods, or having raw sex.

In the next abandoned building, there were a handful of hustlers having either oral sex or serving the addicts their daily doses.

Walking out of that apartment, she saw there was one more abandoned apartment left on the street. Taking a deep breath, a cold shiver ran down her back as she slowly walked through the tarnished blue door. The smell of urine, stale sex, and death assaulted her nose as soon as she walked in.

Oddly, there was not one living soul walking through any of the rooms. When she reached the back room, her heart slammed into her chest. She raised a hand to her chest and looked down at the small, light-skinned girl staring at her through lifeless eyes.

Kneeling, Mercedes pulled Tessa's body into her arms, tears trickling down her face.

"Oh, my God, who did this to you?" she cried, rocking her sister.

Getting to her feet, she struggled to lift Tessa's petite frame. Taking small steps, she made it to the front door and opened it.

Brainiac, who happened to be walking past, saw Mercedes carrying Tessa and ran over.

"What happened to her?" she asked, raising her hand to her mouth.

"I don't know, but I got to call the cops! I can't believe somebody did this shit to her!"

Mercedes cried, moving to step off the porch.

Grabbing Mercedes by her wrist, Brainiac shook her head force-

fully and hopped in front of her, preventing her from taking another step. "You can't do that; you got to leave her here."

"What the fuck you mean?"

"You know exactly what I mean. Sugar doesn't want any of that attention on her business. She told all three of y'all when y'all stepped into this business that y'all were playing a risky game. It's sad to say, but something was bound to happen to her. Shit, something is bound to happen to all of us! You got to take her back in there, Mercedes. Calling the cops ain't too smart, girl," she warned.

"But I can't leave her in there like this! She's my sister!"

"Girl, if you're going to be in this game, you got to learn how to move the fuck on! I had a lot of friends die before my very eyes in these streets and I learned to move on and say fuck it."

"I want my sister back," Mercedes cried, her knees buckling.

Brainiac sighed. After glancing around to see if the coast was clear, she pulled her cell phone out of her bra and dialed 9-1-1, and reported a dead body.

"Okay, they'll be here in a few, so hurry up and put her back in there and be out. I'll meet you back at Sugar's," Brainiac said, walking away.

Mercedes nodded, hot tears burning her cheek. She ran her fingers through Tessa's dead hair as she laid her limp body back onto the mattress.

"I love you, Tessa. We'll always be sisters," she whispered before standing to her feet to leave.

She glanced back one last time, blowing her a kiss, knowing she'd just made one of the hardest decisions in her life.

When she arrived back at Sugar's with her mind, heart, and soul heavy, she dragged her feet into her room, and threw herself onto the bed, her chest heaving and eyes watering. She placed her pillow over her head and screamed into it angrily. Remembering

the image of Tessa's lifeless eyes, she released a low, heart-wrenching scream.

After blowing off steam, she threw the pillow to the other side of the bedroom and exhaled. Knowing she had to get up and prepare to get on the corner, she dragged herself to the closet and collapsed to the floor. With red eyes, she reached into the closet and pulled out her duffle bag and removed a mini dress she'd be rocking that night. As she unfolded the dress, a small card fell to the floor. Picking the card up, she saw the name "Officer Raynisha Williams" with a number printed on it.

"Officer Raynisha Williams? Who's that?" she asked no one in particular.

Snapping her fingers, she remembered Officer Williams as the woman whom she'd met at the police station when she and Corrine had stolen from Giant Eagle.

She did say I could call her whenever I needed her, she thought, holding the card to her mouth, contemplating her next move.

Knowing she didn't have anywhere or anyone to turn to and feeling at her lowest point, her best bet was to give the police-woman a call. If anything, deep down, she hoped it was a sign from God. Picking up the home phone from off of her dresser, she slowly dialed the number that was printed on the card.

"Hello?" a soft, angelic voice answered after the second ringer.

"Hey, I'm looking for Officer Williams."

"This is she; may I ask who's speaking?"

"Mercedes."

"Mercedes who? How did you get my number?"

"Mercedes Owens. Several months ago me and my sister got caught stealing at the Giant Eagle, remember? The foster kids?"

The phone went silent and Mercedes fidgeted, biting her nails, hoping the officer remembered her.

"Oh, yeah! I've been waiting for your call. What took you so long to contact me, Mercedes? And where is Corrine?"

"I don't know, she's—"

"Look, I'm kind of busy right now, but can I come and get you from somewhere in an hour or so? I'd like to catch up and see how you been doing," Officer Williams said sincerely.

"Um..."

"You can trust me, girl; I'm not going to hurt you. Where are you?"

"Up Northview."

"What part? Can I meet you in an hour?"

"On the top of Penfort Street, and I guess so," Mercedes said hesitantly.

"I'll be there." Officer Williams ended the call.

An hour later, Mercedes stood on the corner of Penfort Street, her hair pulled back into a ponytail and dressed in a jogging suit. A midnight-blue car pulled up in front of her and honked. Looking in, she saw a dark-skinned woman who wore a short, cropped hairstyle, in the driver's seat.

"C'mon, girl!" Officer Williams said, waving at Mercedes.

Mercedes hesitantly opened the door and got in.

"Put your seat belt on, girl. And sorry I took so long. I was just getting off work when you called. Is everything okay?" she asked, driving off.

Mercedes nodded and looked out of the window. She remained quiet, noticing a couple and three young children cooking on a grill, laughing, and having a good time. She sighed, wishing she'd had a chance to experience that type of feeling with Tessa and Corrine.

"Are you hungry?"

"Yes."

"Well, I have some lasagna cooking at my place. You don't mind if we go there, do you?"

Mercedes shook her head, still staring out of the window. She remained quiet the rest of the ride to Officer Williams' small brownstone home. Going in, the aroma of the tasty food filled their noses. Mercedes took a seat on the couch and fidgeted, watching Officer Williams take off her jacket and then walk over to her.

Looking into the young girl's sorrowful eyes, she couldn't help but wonder what she'd been through. "What's going on, baby girl? Is everything okay?" she asked, taking a seat next to her.

Mercedes nodded quickly as she looked at the floor. Gently grabbing Mercedes' chin, she lifted it until her eyes met hers. "Young lady, you're too beautiful to be holding your head down. When you're around me and anyone else, I want you to hold that up. You'll mess around and miss a blessing holding your head that low."

Mercedes nodded again and tried to hold her head high.

"Now, I know you wanted something or you wouldn't have called me. What's going on?"

A tear escaped from her eye as Mercedes shook her head, lowering it into her hands. Catching Officer Williams off-guard, she let out a low scream. Officer Williams rubbed her back, allowing her to get any emotion she had held within her out. When she finally stopped crying and caught her breath, Officer Williams reached into her purse, pulled out a tissue, and handed it to her.

"Thank you, Officer," Mercedes said, blowing her nose.

"Please, call me Raynisha. What's going on? Please talk to me."

"This is weird, but I needed someone to talk to and had no one to turn to," Mercedes said, her voice barely above a whisper.

"Sweetie, this doesn't have to be weird." Raynisha smiled kindly.

"I told you before at the police station that I wanted to help you and your sister. I could tell by looking at the both of you that y'all have been through some things."

"I know, I want the pain to go away. I want to be happy."

"And you can be, baby girl. There are always things you can do in life to be happy. It's up to you. You have to take steps and watch everything come in slow; it doesn't happen overnight. Now, tell me what's on your mind?"

Taking a deep breath, Mercedes turned to face Raynisha. She mustered up all the strength and courage she had left and told her everything. She told her about the situation with Rachael abusing her, Corrine, and Tessa. Then, she told her about her prostituting, Corrine's and Tessa's drug addiction, and Tessa's recent death.

Raynisha raised a hand to her chest, looking at the broken young woman before her. She wrapped her arms around Mercedes, giving her a warm hug, silently assuring her everything would be fine.

"I knew there was something about you that had me drawn to you when I first met you, but I couldn't put my finger on it," Raynisha finally said.

"What do you mean?"

"When I was younger, I was also in a foster care and ran away after being abused by my foster father. He'd molested and raped me for over ten years."

"Are you serious? What did you do about it?"

"I ran away, girl. I got into drugs, partying, and everything."

"Really? I would never have thought that," Mercedes said, appalled.

"Me either. But, after almost dying in them streets, I got myself together. I got my GED, went into law, and became a police officer. That's what I mean, because you've been through a lot of

things in life doesn't mean you can't or won't ever be happy. You have to fight for it, baby girl. Life is too short. You have to stand for something or you will fall for anything. Everything worth having is worth fighting for; remember that."

"You're right, Raynisha. I never thought I'd ever sink this low, though. I can't believe my sister is gone. I tried to save her from sinking in these streets. But no matter what I did, it never worked."

"You can't beat yourself up about it, Mercedes. You're still young and you have the whole world ahead of you. You have to learn how to let go and let God, girl. And the first step of this is to stop prostituting," Raynisha said.

"I can't, Raynisha, I can't. I don't have anywhere to go, and that's my only income."

"Listen, you have me now. Matter of fact, I want you and Corrine to stay with me. Maybe this was meant to happen. Maybe God sent you to me for a given reason. You see what happened to your sister; you don't want you or Corrine to be next."

Tears filled Mercedes' eyes. Overwhelmed with emotion, she didn't know what her next move would be. She knew from the sincerity in Raynisha's voice that she was a woman of her word, but she didn't want to depend on someone else.

"Okay, I have an idea," she said.

"I'm listening."

"I'm going to continue to prostitute for two more weeks. I have seventeen thousand dollars saved up and my goal was twenty. In two weeks, I should reach my goal. When that happens, I'll take my and Corrine's things, pack them up, and head over here."

"You have seventeen thousand, why be greedy, girl? You are under-aged and prostituting, at that. Who are you working for? I'm sorry, Mercedes, but I can't allow you to continue to do this."

"Please, Raynisha? I been doing this for months and twenty

was a goal I wanted to reach. Plus, I don't ever like depending on anyone. If I touch twenty, I'll be good to take care of me and Corrine until we finally get back on our feet. I promise, two more weeks and I'm done," Mercedes pleaded.

Throwing her arms up in surrender, Raynisha said, "I'm serious, Mercedes, I want to see both of you off of those streets in two weeks. If I don't, I will have to turn the both of you in, do you understand?"

"Yes, I understand."

CHAPTER TWENTY ONE

"You get any info on that bitch yet?" Respect asked Jewels.

They were both in Jewels' condominium, counting their week's profit. It'd been over a month since they'd been back on the streets, and things were slowly but surely coming back into place for all of them.

He looked at the tall piles of money stacked on the living room table and took another pull from his sweet cigar. "Yep, she lives with that bitch, Sugar. Sugar be having her posted on the corner of Hazlet and shit. If we're lucky, we could probably catch her tonight."

"Do you want me or that nigga Brooke to go with you? I got some business to tend to tonight."

"I'll call Brooke; handle your business," Jewels said, putting his cigar out in his ashtray.

He sat down and leaned back in his chair, looking at the stacked money. *Yeah, this is what the fuck I'm talking about. Life is good*, he thought.

"Hey, Daddy," Yazmin yelled, running into the room.

"Hey, baby girl; I didn't even know you were awake. You hungry?" he asked.

"Yes, but where's Mommy, Daddy? When is she coming home from her vacation?"

Staring into her eyes, he couldn't help but think of how much

of Relisha's features his daughter had inherited from her. Even though he'd killed Relisha, he couldn't help but think about her every day since she was the mother of his only child. Deep down, he regretted murdering her, but, on the flip side, she had the same blood running through her body as his archenemy, and that he could no longer accept.

"She'll be home soon, baby. Now go back into the living room while Daddy cooks for you, okay?"

Yazmin nodded and ran back into the living room. It pained him that he would have to lie to his daughter for the rest of her life about her mother, but if that's what he had to do to prevent her from knowing the truth, that's exactly what he'd do.

✠ ✠ ✠

"You got fifty dollars on you, bro?" Day'onne asked Menace.

He, Menace, and Troy sat on Menace's couch, drinking alcohol and smoking marijuana. Menace, who once lived in a luxurious mansion, now resorted to moving back up Northview. His place was a live disaster, filled with trash scattered everywhere on the floor and a deadly stench. His apartment wasn't a far cry from when he was younger, living in his mother's house. They both had the same, spoiled food smell, dirty floors that needed a good mop job, and barely any furniture to make it feel like a home.

"No, bro. You know I'm broke as hell. I want another bottle of that Dom P, though."

Day'onne shook his head and dug into his pockets, finding a ten-dollar bill in one and a one in the other.

"Damn, I only got eleven stinky-ass dollars on me? This shit is a shame! We need to get back out there, bro!" Day'onne yelled in a drunken slur.

"With what fucking money? We don't even have fifty dollars on us!" Troy said.

Day'onne shook his head again and sunk down into the couch, holding an empty bottle of Ciroc.

The place he was in his life now felt like a nightmare. Not even able to afford a bottle of alcohol, he didn't think he could sink any lower. Only two months ago, he'd been on top of the world, blowing money and living the fast life.

"Man, I don't give a fuck what y'all talking, Pittsburgh still my motherfucking city! I'm known in these fucking streets to wreak havoc!" he spat viciously.

"Man, whatever." Troy laughed. "Fuck it, we might as well deal with it, we broke as hell! Not everybody gets to stay on top for long!"

Jumping to his feet, his eyes bucking, Day'onne threw the empty bottle to the floor and screamed, "Broke? Nigga, speak for yourself. I'm never broke, man. I'll kill a bitch or nigga for calling me broke."

Menace and Troy laughed hysterically, watching him kick empty bottles around like a madman.

"Bro, it's cool; we'll get back on our shit," Menace finally said, trying to calm his best friend.

"Fuck yeah, we will! And I'll do whatever it takes!" Day'onne vowed.

CHAPTER TWENTY TWO

Corrine sat in the corner of her bedroom with her legs glued to her chest and her arms wrapped around them, rocking back and forth, shaking. She wiped her runny nose with the back of her hand and scratched her dry, ashy neck. Her body was going through withdrawal. It'd been more than three days since she'd had her last dose of cocaine and she was craving for it.

She needed to get her "medicine" soon and she'd vowed she'd do anything to get it. But ever since she got addicted to drugs and lost all of her drop-dead gorgeous physique, Corrine also had lost most of her clients. But deciding to beat the odds, she finally got to her feet before she walked out of the room. Her knees wobbled as she used the wall as her support and walked downstairs. When she reached the bottom of the steps, she bumped right into Sugar.

"I hope you're on your way to make my money, little girl. Because I'm telling you, if your ass don't have my money, you're out of here," Sugar snapped, grabbing Corrine by her collar and poking her in the forehead.

She nodded and made her way out of the house. On Hazlet Street, onlookers laughed when she licked her cracked, chapped lips and took a rubber band from around her wrist, folded her dirty T-shirt under her small breasts, and tied it. After standing on the corner for twenty minutes, a black Escalade pulled up in front

of her and she got excited. She sashayed to the passenger side of the car, putting an extra switch in her walk and forcing a smile.

"Hey, papi, you ready for a good time?" Corrine asked, her voice cracking.

Jewels, who was in the driver's seat, nodded and flashed a fake smile to mask his disgust. Corrine hopped into the passenger's seat and before she had a good chance to close the door, she was already fumbling with his crotch.

"Damn, ma, hold up. Trust me, you'll have plenty of time for that." Jewels laughed.

She rolled her eyes and folded her arms under her breasts when he finally drove out of Northview.

Brooke, who was in the backseat of the SUV, discreetly drenched a folded washcloth with chloroform. Corrine was too focused on turning her next client to notice Brooke slide out of the backseat, kneel, and wrap his muscular hands around her mouth. Her eyes bucked when he placed the cloth against her nose and tightly held it there. She tried clawing at his hands but she became weak, losing consciousness moments later.

✠ ✠ ✠

"Hello, son," Ms. Younger said, opening the front door to allow Deion to walk in.

As usual, he was clean-shaven and dressed in a Adidas jogging suit with matching tennis shoes.

He and Ms. Younger hadn't seen or talked to each other since their argument when she'd kicked him out of her house. With all he was dealing with, it was finally time to go see and talk to the only person who'd loved him unconditionally for the past several years.

"Hey, Ms. Younger," he said, walking into the kitchen.

"So, how have you been? Have you taken my advice?"

"I've been good, low-key lately. And yes, I have. I don't know what I was thinking," Deion admitted, holding his head low.

Placing her hand under his chin, Ms. Younger gently lifted his head. "Baby, don't be so hard on yourself, we all make mistakes. Like everyone else, I want the best for you. I love you, boy. I would hate to see something happen to you while you're out there on those streets, Deion. I wanted to teach you a lesson."

"And lesson learned, Ms. Younger. I was so caught up in the money and fast life, I didn't take heed that my decisions were affecting everyone else. But it's all good, I'm completely out of the game. I want to focus on my writing again and finding my little sister, Corrine."

Ms. Younger's eyes beamed in excitement when he mentioned Corrine's name. She had been waiting for the day that he would finally look for his long-lost sister.

Even though she didn't know her and had never met her, she was his family and that was the most important thing.

"Really? What made you finally want to find her?"

"I had a long talk with an old friend, Jarell. He convinced me. I want to reunite with her and apologize for never being there for her."

Taking a deep breath, Deion shook his head, his mind drifting back.

"Why haven't you ever been there for her? What was really stopping you?"

"When I was sixteen, Day'onne raped Corrine. She asked me, begged me, not to tell Melissa, and I agreed. All this time, I've felt so guilty for never telling Melissa, that I never wanted to look at Corrine. Every time I looked at her, my mind would rewind

to the day he raped her and I couldn't do anything to prevent it. I felt too guilty," Deion finally admitted.

Ms. Younger wiped the tear that ran down Deion's cheek before wrapping her arms around him and giving him a tight hug. She cupped her hands around his face. "So, that explains why you didn't want to see her. In eight years, Deion? You've got to let that go, baby. That was the past. Neglecting your family isn't going to solve anything. You've got to learn how to quit running from your problems and face them. The time is now, Deion. You have to stop running from Corrine and finally face her."

Deion nodded in agreement as he wiped his tears away. "I know and—"

The loud ringing of his cell phone interrupted him. Taking it out of his pocket, he looked at the screen and saw it was someone calling from a private number.

"Who's this?" Deion answered.

"What's up, Deion?"

"I asked you who this is?"

"Don't worry about that. All I want you to worry about is saving your crackheaded little sister. Now, I want you to listen to me and I want you to listen closely, you understand?"

Sitting down, the color drained from Deion's face and he felt his esophagus closing in. His breathing became heavy and his eye twitched. Seeing the fear in his face, Ms. Younger became concerned but remained quiet.

"On the east side in Homewood, I want you to drop off two hundred thousand dollars, in cash. There will be an abandoned building right by the bus station and that's where I want you to put the money. You have four hours to make this happen, Deion. I got your precious little sister right here, and I know you don't want anything to happen to her, now do you?" Jewels said.

"No, I'll have the money."

"That's what I like to hear. Like I said, you have four hours. I'll keep in contact," Jewels said, ending the call.

Deion slammed the phone down onto the table and laid his head into his hands.

"If it isn't one thing, it's another, man!" he cried.

"Baby, what's going on?" Ms. Younger asked with concern.

"They have Corrine! They want two hundred thousand or she's dead!"

"Who has her? Why do they have her?"

"I think it's a man named Jewels. Remember I was telling you about him? Ever since Day'onne robbed him when we were younger, he never seems to go away. But I have to go, I got to go save Corrine," Deion said, flaring his nose and standing to his feet.

"But wait, baby! Where are you going to get all of that money from? I don't want you to do anything dangerous, Deion!" Ms. Younger cried.

"I still got money saved up from the book. I'll give them all of that. And this is my only chance, Ms. Younger. I've never been there for Corrine before, but I'll damn sure be there for her now! She's family and she needs me."

With that, he left, slamming the door behind him, leaving Ms. Younger speechless.

Returning to his condominium, Deion stormed into his bedroom and flipped his mattress to retrieve the .9mm that Day'onne had given him a couple months prior.

Reaching under the bed, he pulled out a box labeled *Hustling Hard* and opened it. In it was over three hundred thousand dollars he'd retrieved from his book royalties. He counted off two hundred thousand dollars and placed it in a duffle bag he got from the closet. Grabbing the bag, he jetted out to his car and headed to Northview.

✠✠✠

Mercedes stood on her usual corner on Penfort, dressed in a burnt-orange sleeveless dress. It was eleven o'clock and she promised herself the next customer would be her last for the night. She closed her eyes tightly as the cold, bitter winter wind assaulted her bare skin as she rubbed her hands together to keep them warm. When she opened her eyes again, she saw a black BMW approaching. Standing tall, she arched her back and made her legs go inward, making herself appear bowlegged.

When the man behind the wheel flashed his headlights twice, she sashayed to the passenger's seat and smiled. Hopping into the car, she said, "What's up, daddy? What you—"

The man with sleek the temple fade and slanted eyes caused her words to get caught in her throat. She glared at him and tried to open the door, but he had already locked it.

"Please, don't go anywhere, I need your help!" Deion pleaded, grabbing her wrist.

"What the fuck do you want?" she spat, snatching away from him.

Taking a deep breath, he shook his head and a single tear slipped from one eye. "Look, Corrine is in danger. I came to you because you two are close and I need your help. I can't do this alone."

"What do you mean, she's in danger?"

"About two hours ago, I got a call from some man demanding two hundred thousand dollars for Corrine, or else."

"Or else, what? Who's this man?"

"Look, I don't have time to discuss all of it, girl. All you need to know is that Corrine needs our help, and I know she's counting on someone to help her."

"Our help? Since when did you start caring about her? Last

time I checked, you haven't seen that girl in years and didn't give one fuck about her! Why the fuck do you care now?" Mercedes asked harshly.

"Because she's family—"

"Family? I'm the only family she got! You haven't seen that girl in over what? Eight years? And now you're screaming *family*? Get the fuck out of here! I'll help you, but please know I'm only doing this for her, not you."

"I deserve that, but that's all I ask, Mercedes. She needs both of us," Deion said, pulling off.

Mercedes shook her head in disbelief and folded her arms under her chest.

"If it isn't one thing, it's another."

"So tell me because I've been dying to know, why did you do this to Corrine? What has she done to you to make you act as if she never existed?"

"It's a long story, Mercedes. But I'm here now; isn't that all that matters?" Deion asked sincerely.

"I guess so, Deion. I'm surprised that you popped up out of the blue, wanting to be in your sister's life. She's been through a lot and she's losing it. But I guess you're right; you're here now and that's all that matters."

They remained quiet until Deion pulled up in front of his designated destination and got out of the car.

"Where are we?"

"At my brother's. Stay close to me and put this on," Deion instructed, taking off his leather jacket and handing it to her.

She nodded her head and she slipped the jacket on and followed close behind him. Walking into Day'onne's safe house—a small, roach-infested apartment—he wrinkled up his nose. Mercedes' mind instantly rewound back to the time when she, Corrine, and

Tessa lived with Rachael. She cupped her hands over her nose, trying to muffle out the vicious odor. When they walked into the living room, they found Day'onne and Menace on the couch, high out of their minds.

"Yo, Day'onne, get the fuck up!" Deion yelled angrily, shaking Day'onne.

Day'onne, who had smoked at least five blunts and drunk a whole bottle by himself, smiled goofily up at Deion.

"What's good, bro?" He snickered.

"Yo, I need your help, bro. Corrine's in trouble!" Deion yelled.

"Man, fuck that bitch!"

"Fuck you mean? Nigga, get the fuck up, man! She needs us!"

Day'onne waved him off, taking a liquor bottle off of the table and taking a swig from it. Angry, Deion walked back out of the apartment with Mercedes following him.

"Did you say his name was Day'onne?"

"Yeah, that's my twin brother. I wanted him to help us out with this shit since he's the source of the problem. But fuck it, I guess we got to do it ourselves." Deion kept walking.

So he's the one that raped Corrine, Mercedes thought as they hopped back into his car.

Deion started his ignition and pulled off.

CHAPTER TWENTY THREE

Feeling hands assaulting her, Corrine opened her eyes.

They had her stashed in one of their old trap houses. The dirty place reeked of decomposed bodies, fish, and burned flesh.

She was sprawled out on a dirty abandoned apartment floor, beaten to a bloody pulp, her breath becoming short gasps. Her eyes were almost swollen shut and her naturally supple lips looked like golf balls on her face. Her body ached and she continued to go through withdrawal, yearning for a dose of cocaine.

Gathering the little strength she had within, she managed to say, "Please stop."

Jewels wickedly laughed as he ripped her clothes off and pulled down his pants.

He spat on his fingers and wiped it on Corrine's opening, then grabbed the base of his fat, nasty penis and roughly plunged it into her. Corrine arched her back in pain and released a loud scream, trying to squirm out of the tight grip he had on her. Tormented, she cried from the pain that continued to taunt at her young body as Jewels continued to rape her.

"Damn, your shit feel just like Relisha's!" Jewels panted as he continued to pound her insides.

Jewels laughed as he kneeled down, forcing his tongue down her throat. Hot tears continued to burn her cheek as she tried to escape, but it was to no avail.

"Oh, shit!" Jewels moaned, ejaculating on her stomach.

Jewels stood up and pulled his pants back up. Corrine curled into a fetal position, paralyzed with pain. For the first time in a very long time, she wished she was in Mercedes' arms, letting her know everything would be okay.

"Bitch, we're not done with you!" Brooke yelled, grabbing hold of her hair.

She let out out a bloodcurdling scream as he dragged her back and forth like a mop in the abandoned apartment. Brooke continued to beat her like she was nothing; less than a human being. He stomped, punched, and even pistol-whipped her with the butt of his gun.

Lying in a pool of her own blood and watching her whole life flash before her, she lost faith in life.

"Just kill me...please," she pleaded weakly.

✠ ✠ ✠

"When do you think they'll call?" Mercedes asked Deion, taking a sip from her can of soda.

"I don't know, they should be calling any minute now," he said, glancing at his platinum Rolex.

They were seated on Deion's couch, watching television, and waiting for the right time to deliver the money, in which they had an hour left. Mercedes was dressed in a pair of black sweat pants, black Chuck Taylor sneakers, and a black pullover hoodie. Her hair was tied into a tight ponytail and she had not one speck of makeup. Deion was also dressed in all black. He had on a black sweat suit, black Timberland boots, and an all-black Pittsburgh Pirates snap-back cap. He looked at Mercedes, admiring her dark, smooth skin, feisty attitude, and even her grind. Taking her by the hand, he softly said, "I'm sorry you and Corrine had to go

through the things y'all went through. I can tell by looking in your eyes that you've been through a lot. But I want to tell you now, I really want to get to know my younger sister all over again, and I promise you I won't ever neglect her again."

"That was random; where did that come from?"

"Nowhere; I'm sitting here thinking, that's all. I wanted you to know that."

"Well, I'm glad to hear that. I hope Corrine accepts you back into her life. She's been through a lot and, like me, she wants to be happy."

"Yeah, I want both of you to be happy, too. I swear when we get out of this predicament, I'm going to be the best brother I can possibly be," he vowed.

"Let me ask you something?" Mercedes said, taking her hands out of his and turning her body so she was completely facing him.

"Shoot."

"Your twin, did he really rape Corrine?"

Caught off-guard by the question, Deion gasped. He looked down for a moment, raised his head, and nodded. "Yeah, when we were much younger."

"And you knew this? Why didn't you help her?"

"I don't know; I really couldn't do anything to help."

"What do you mean, you couldn't do anything to help? That's your sister, you're sup—"

The loud ringing of Deion's cell phone prevented Mercedes from uttering another word. Seeing it was a private call, he eagerly flipped his cell phone open.

"Hello?"

"I hope you're ready?" Jewels said.

"Yeah, I got your money. Where is my sister?" Deion said, clenching his jaw.

Removing the cell phone from his ear, Jewels placed the phone

to Corrine's mouth and she moaned. He slightly smiled before placing the phone back to his ear. "Did you hear that?"

"Yeah. What did you do to her? If you hurt her, I swear—"

"I don't think it's too smart for you to be making threats to me right now, don't you agree? I want you to deliver the money, now. You have less than an hour," Jewels said before hanging up.

"Okay, he's ready. Let's go," Deion said to Mercedes, jumping to his feet and grabbing his car keys off the table.

Less than thirty minutes later, they arrived in Homewood. It was a little after midnight and the streets were unusually quiet, not one soul walking the lonely street. When they reached their destination, he turned to Mercedes. "Okay, I want you to stay in here and be on lookout while I deliver this money."

"What if they come after me? I don't have any protection on me!" Mercedes said, worried.

Reaching into his glove compartment, Deion pulled out a .357 and handed it to her. She held the metal in her hands, ready to bust a move on anyone.

"You sure you'll be okay with that? Do you know how to use it?"

"Yeah, I got this, don't worry about me. Just be careful, I got your back," Mercedes assured him.

Deion nodded and got out, gripping his .9mm. Carrying the heavy duffle bag filled with the ransom money, he looked around, making sure nothing was out of the ordinary. When he reached the abandoned apartment, as instructed, he walked in and threw the bag onto the floor. Taking a deep breath, he walked back out and made his way back toward his car.

✠ ✠ ✠

"He did it," Brooke said.

He and Jewels had kept Corrine hostage in another abandoned

building across the street so they could see whether or not Deion. Brooke had been watching from a window the entire time.

"I'll be right back, I'm going to go get it," Brooke said as he made his way to the door.

"I'll be watching. Hurry up and get back," Jewels said.

When Brooke entered the abandoned apartment where Deion had dropped the money off, he didn't notice the BMW following him.

Deion, who'd never left the area, watched through his tinted windows. When he'd seen Brooke leaving the building and going across the street to the abandoned apartment, he instantly knew who he was.

Putting his car in PARK, he hopped back out of the car and made his way toward Brooke inside the building.

"So, y'all bitch-ass niggas really thought y'all was really going to get away with this?" Deion said, pointing his .9mm at Brooke.

Caught off-guard, Brooke dropped the duffle bag filled with money, reached for his waistband, but cursed himself, realizing he'd left his gun in the room with Jewels and Corrine.

"Fuck you, bitch-ass nigga!" Brooke spat. "If you going to kill me, you might as well do it now."

"Any last words?"

"That crackheaded bitch's pussy was bomb!" Brooke laughed.

Gripped with anger, Deion wasted no time pulling the trigger, earning his first body. With not one ounce of regret, he watched as Brooke's lifeless body collapsed to the ground.

Jewels heard the gunshots coming from the abandoned building and looked out of the window.

"Oh shit! What the fuck?" he yelled, pulling out his Desert Eagle.

He glanced at Corrine who sat bound to a chair, beaten beyond recognition.

She sat there in a daze, praying to God to end her life. She knew death was knocking at her door and she embraced it, thinking it was better than suffering.

Standing, Jewels headed for the door. Before walking out of the dirty room, he cocked his gun and pulled the trigger, pumping one hot bullet into her chest.

Deion walked out of the front door of the apartment and saw a big, beastly figure running toward him. Without a second thought, he raised his gun and pulled the trigger.

"Where the fuck is Corrine?" he asked, continuing to shoot.

Jewels ducked and dodged every bullet as he also started to let off rounds.

"That bitch dead, nigga!" Jewels laughed as he continued to shoot, which only infuriated Deion.

Blinded by rage, he ran out of the abandoned building in a blur. Before Jewels could grasp the whole situation, Deion charged at him, knocking him to the ground while his gun skidded several inches away from them. Now on top of Jewels, he drew his hand back and delivered a hard blow to his face. He continued to hit him in his face until Jewels grabbed hold of his wrists and bent them backward. Wincing, he then started to get off of Jewels, to retrieve his gun, but Jewels stopped him. The two men began to tussle for the gun, kicking and punching at each other. Struggling to get the upper hand, Deion tried his best to use his body weight on the oversized Jewels, but it was to no avail.

"Yeah, nigga!" Jewels growled when we finally got hold of the gun.

Like the man he was, Deion looked Jewels in the eyes, willing to accept his fate. But before Jewels even had the chance to pull the trigger, Mercedes walked up behind him, placed her .357 to his head, and pulled the trigger.

Deion watched as Jewels stared him in the eyes as he lifelessly

fell to the ground. Breathing heavily, they rushed to the apartment where they'd seen Brooke and Jewels leave from.

They crashed through the front door and the stench of death overpowered them. In the dark living room, Deion saw the silhouette of a girl sitting in a chair.

He exhaled, mentally preparing himself for the worst. Seeing a flashlight on the floor, he picked it up and turned it on.

"Oh, God, what did they do to you?" he cried, dropping to the floor.

The sight of his younger sister, bound, naked, beaten, and with a bullet lodged in her chest, was too much for him to take. Crying, Mercedes untied the ropes from around Corrine's chest, and her limp body fell into her arms. Deion got to his feet, looking at the young girl he hadn't seen in eight years.

Gently picking her up, he carried her out and placed her in the back of his car. Still crying, Mercedes climbed in with her, running her fingers through her hair. Pulling off, Deion headed to the nearest hospital.

CHAPTER TWENTY FOUR

Deion and Mercedes sat next to Corrine's hospital bed. She'd been in a coma for a month and they were patiently waiting for her to wake up.

Mercedes was dressed in a pair of straight-leg blue jean pants, a hot-pink blouse, and a pair of hot-pink leather boots. Her wavy hair hung down her back and gold eye shadow accentuated her dark, flawless skin. Dressed in his usual jogging suit, Deion was asleep, snoring softly. Crossing her legs, Mercedes slowly folded her arms under her breasts and looked at Corrine. After going through many major surgeries for over a month, Mercedes and the rest of them were praying for her health to increase.

"Hey, girl!" Raynisha walked into the hospital room smiling, dressed in her police uniform and carrying a bouquet of flowers.

"Hey, Ray. You bought these for her? These are beautiful!" Mercedes smiled before giving her a welcoming hug.

"Yeah, girl. Wow, he's knocked clean out." Raynisha laughed, nodding at Deion.

Mercedes took the bouquet out of her hands before putting it on a nearby table where the rest of the "Get Well Soon" balloons and other flowers were located. Staring down at Corrine, Mercedes smiled. Turning back to face Raynisha, Mercedes took a seat next to her.

"I'm sorry I haven't really been home lately. I've been in the

library studying to pass my GED classes and visiting her, so things have been a little hectic lately," Mercedes said.

"Girl, it's fine. Don't stress it. I'm glad that you're out of those streets, living with me, and back in school. Look at you, Mercedes. You're glowing! What did I tell you?"

"Let go and let God," they said in unison, bursting into a soft laughter.

"Raynisha. I can't believe it, either. I wish Tessa was here to see me now. But I know she's looking down at me and smiling right about now. And once Corrine gets out of here, I swear I'll do everything in my power to keep her off the streets and off of those drugs."

"Oh, yeah, I'll make sure she stays off those streets, too. Even if it takes all the strength in my body, this little girl will make it. I've already taken action and been appointed her legal guardian, so don't worry about her. You need to worry about yourself now, Mercedes. Have you thought about what you want to do with your life whenever you get your GED?"

"Yes, I want to go to school to be a sonogram technician."

"Good, and like I tell you all the time, anything is possible if you put your mind to it."

Mercedes nodded in agreement and turned when Corrine's doctor, Dr. Kennedy, walked into the room.

His bifocal glasses rested on the bridge of his nose as he tilted his head and looked at a chart that he held in his hands. He stared at Corrine, then back at the chart.

"Hello, is there a problem, doctor?" Raynisha asked, frowning.

"Yes, Ms. Williams, we have received the urine test back for Corrine Johnson, and it appears…"

"What? Appears what?"

"Ms. Johnson is four weeks' pregnant."

EPILOGUE
THREE MONTHS LATER...

Corrine weakly stepped out of the black BMW with a cane in her hand. She took baby steps, hesitantly walking toward the Pennsylvania Rehabilitation Center. Feeling hands on her, she stopped.

"Go ahead, baby girl. We're right by your side," Deion assured her with a warm smile.

He stood beside her, gently holding on to her frail arm and guiding her toward her future. Mercedes, who stood on the side of her, and Raynisha, who stood behind her, nodded their heads in agreement.

Corrine, who was dressed in a blue jean outfit that hung loosely on her body, flashed a fragile smile before taking a deep breath, clutched her small, pregnant stomach and continued to walk, but this time with much more confidence. When she finally reached the inside of the rehabilitation center and all three of them let go of her, she turned around, shielded her slanted eyes that now held hope in them, and waved goodbye to the only family she had left in this world.

Deion, now teary-eyed, ran and wrapped his strong, masculine arms around her petite frame, rocking her back and forth. She melted in his arms as he stroked her hair, telling her how much he loved her. Stepping back, he looked his little sister in the eyes. "I love you, baby girl. And I'm sorry for everything."

Remaining silent and giving him a reassuring smile, Corrine nodded before turning around and walking away.

Deion, Mercedes, and Raynisha waved her goodbye for the time being, hoping she'd walked into the center a girl and finally walk out a young woman.

✠ ✠ ✠

An hour later, Deion and Mercedes parted ways with Raynisha and they pulled up in front of an apartment in Northview. The sun was still shining and everyone in the neighborhood was out, enjoying the hot day. Dressed in an all-black cocktail dress and black stiletto pumps, Mercedes sat and stared at the house.

"So, this is where he stays at now?"

"Yeah, do you want me to handle this?"

Shaking her head, she reached into her leather pocketbook and pulled out her small .357. Turning around to face him, she said, "No, I want to do this by myself. I have to."

Getting out of the car, she walked toward the apartment with confidence, her head held high with each step.

Walking onto the porch, to her surprise, she found the front door unlocked. Turning the doorknob, she clutched her gun in her hand and looked around the living room with caution.

She shook her head in disgust and continued to stare around the usual smelly apartment. When she walked upstairs and found a man slumped over on a dirty mattress, she flipped him over.

Day'onne, who was in his usual drunken state of mind and looked like he was in good need of a wash, mumbled to himself and looked confused.

Mercedes turned her nose up and pointed her gun at him. "Big, bad-ass Day'onne, look at you now."

Day'onne, who was too much under the influence, continued to mumble under his breath and tried to stand, but quickly stumbled.

Cocking her gun and pointing it at his head, Mercedes took a deep breath, placing her hand on the trigger. Squinting her eyes, she said, "This is for Corrine."

Pulling the trigger, she watched as Day'onne's lifeless body limply fell to the dirty floor.

Exhaling, she walked out of the dirty room and house. Refusing to look back, she was finally happy to know she had closed that chapter of her life.

✠ ✠ ✠

Shay sat in her red Beemer, clutching her bulging stomach and looking through the windshield. She watched in envy as a beautiful, dark-skinned girl walked out of Day'onne's apartment, hopped into Deion's BMW and pulled off.

Getting out of the car, she walked on the porch and opened the door. A foul stench smacked her against her puffy cheeks, causing her to place her hand over her nose. She made her way up the stairs and into the first bedroom, not prepared for what she was about to see.

She held her swollen stomach as she made it out of the room as fast as she could. Walking into the living room, she doubled over and vomited. When she regained her composure, she walked back into the room and stared down at a lifeless Day'onne.

Turning, she walked out of the apartment and got back in her car. Always devious, she smiled mischievously, already plotting.

ABOUT THE AUTHOR

Paige Green is a high school senior from Pittsburgh, PA, where she grew up in the Northview Heights area. Since the age of 10, she has written plays, short stories, and eventually *Family Over Everything*. Motivated by her surroundings, she pushed herself to always strive for a more. Paige plans to attend college in one of the Southern states where she will major in Literature. Her main goal in life is to help young, at-risk females who are trying to find their way in life. Paige lives with her mother, two older brothers, and twin sister, Paris Green, in the Atlanta area.

IF YOU ENJOYED "FAMILY OVER EVERYTHING," PLEASE BE SURE TO CHECK OUT

LITTLE WHITE LIES

BY COLE RILEY

COMING SOON FROM STREBOR BOOKS

1 / HALLUCINATIONS

FALL 2006

The word around the neighborhood was that I was the good one, the levelheaded, ambitious boy who would make good one day. And never shame the family. I tried to be normal, the quiet nerd, the potential breadwinner. However, that was not to be the case.

My father said I reminded him of Doctor J, Elgin Baylor, Oscar Robertson, and even Michael Jordan when I found the proper stroke, the proper dribble, the proper pass. We used to shoot hoops in the backyard, and later on a tattered basketball court with tufts of grass peeking through the buckled asphalt. School was something I hated. I was never any good with numbers, grammar, or science. But put a basketball in my hands and I was an artist.

A rowdy crowd of supporters turned out to see us topple Cardozo by 12 points, allowing our team to capture a share of the division title. The Cardozo squad was playing without their top sophomore forward, Akim Lawrence, who was nursing a head cold. Still, the red-hot guards almost snatched the victory away in the third quarter with four three-pointers.

"Melvin, this win would mean a lot for our franchise and our school," Ron Faulk, our coach, said to me. "You've shown leadership throughout our entire season and you cannot let us down now. Not now. They're underestimating you and what you bring to our team. Kick some butt, son."

I thought back about how we beat Bishop Ford, Jefferson and even Nazareth. These dudes were a snap for us. I started rebounding and blocking shots, going out and putting my hand in the faces of the slick guards. Coach Faulk called our opposition Heckle and Jeckle, after the TV cartoon crows. Were they magpies?

Our 6-11 center, Houston Crown, stood in our huddle, grabbing me by the arm and speaking in his deep baritone voice. "They're talking a lot of smack out there. They say we're punks, we're chumps. Everybody thinks they can beat us. I take this personal and I know you guys do too."

"Shit, we cannot let them come to our house and talk a lot of shit," Emory Lewis, our point guard said. "We can't let them disrespect us and take the win. We've got to turn it up. We got to put them in their place. Smash-mouth ball, guys, smash-mouth ball."

The only game we lost all season was a blowout with Boys & Girl High in Brooklyn. They kicked our asses. I knew our team was better than that. I was real emotional 'bout that game. The reason I was not in the line-up was back spasms; it hurt to move, much less run up and down the court. Now, the guys were count-

ing on me, looking at me and weighing whether I was up to the task.

Coach Faulk watched as one of the magpies shot the ball at the top of the key and it rimmed out. He called time out and we ran toward the sidelines in our snazzy red and black uniforms. All eyes were on me. The coach diagramed a play calling for me to shoot a jumper at the corner.

"We got to settle down," the coach said in a drained whisper. "Don't rush the shots. Play methodically. Focus. We got to put the ball in the hands of Melvin and he'll take care of business. Won't you, Melvin?"

I nodded. I shot the jumper but one of their players got a hard foul on me as I was going up with the ball. The ball went in on the foul shot, but the second one came out and bounced into the hands of the opposition.

The enemy called a time-out. We watched them and their coach, a loudmouth usually playing to the cameras. He gestured wildly and angrily, and slapped one of the boys on the back. They came back out and tried to do the play, which we stopped dead in its tracks. Emory picked off the pass and outran the speedy magpies to do a weak lay-up. Each team had another shot to end the game in regulation, until I put in a contested jumper as time expired.

They lifted me on their shoulders and carried me to the locker room. Spectators were pouring out of the stands, yelling and screaming my name. I felt damn good. As I was getting dressed, Coach Faulk smiled and said the sky was the limit for me. Emory walked past me and said we're going out to celebrate tonight.

I figured we had one game left to play, a brawl with St. Peter's Prep, and that would be a warm-up for the City Finals. Tonight, I'd act a total fool. I didn't want to think about how I got hurt

during the game with Westinghouse just a year ago. One of the opposing players tangled my leg in his, maybe intentionally, as we went up for a rebound and I was writhing on the wood floor, unable to get up.

"Are you hurt, son?" my coach asked me. "Can you get up? Do you think you can get off the court unassisted?"

He was giving me a way out, to bravely get back up and trot off the court like a warrior. However, I felt like a punk, a sissy. Something had given away in my leg and my ankle when I fell. I felt it pull and later it burned like hell.

"Can you get up?" Coach Faulk wanted to do the right thing.

"Dammit, I don't think I can," I whined.

In no time, the coach waved over the trainers, who knelt beside me and manipulated my leg, then my ankle. All on the left side. I grimaced with pain and tried to hide my face with my shirt so the rest of the team wouldn't see how much I was suffering with this damn thing.

The coach whispered to the chief trainer in an urgent voice, gripping him on the arm. "Do you think he'll be able to play tonight?"

"Not in this game," the trainer replied. The arena was hushed while they waited to see if I would leave the court under my own power. I was lifted up, between two burly players and carried to the bench. Some of the team's admirers clapped and hooted while those in the know reserved their applause to see how badly I was hurt.

After the game, which we lost by eight points, I was told that I had a bad left mid-ankle sprain but there was nothing seriously wrong with my leg. When the doctor and the chief trainer told me the good news after I was X-rayed at the hospital, I was overjoyed. Coach Faulk said I would probably be out a week or two.

They wrapped my ankle tightly, gave me some painkillers, and sent me home.

"You gave a good acting job out there," my father hissed. He was always pushing me, pushing me. "You could have got up if you wanted to. You acted like a punk."

"Don't call me that," I protested. "The trainer said I hurt my ankle and that was that. The coach didn't want me to play."

"It's because of you that the team lost the game. You know that."

I shouted at him angrily. "That's not true!"

He smiled cruelly. "You punked out. You punked out when they needed you most. How does that feel, knowing that you didn't give your all?"

I turned from him and hobbled on my crutches to my room. My father was still yelling and ranting about how much of a coward I was, so I drowned him out with some jams from Biggie and Tupac. I knew how much he hated rap. Nigger baboon music, he called it.

"Turn that shit down," he screamed. "Turn that fuckin' shit down. Don't let me have to come in there. I'll knock the damn hell out of you."

I put on some headphones and listened to the music. There was something about him that reminded me about Drake Rice, whose father had high hopes for him as well. Drake's daddy was convinced he was going to play in the NBA and be a superstar. Just like Wilt or Bill Russell. My own father had those same damn dreams; one of many men living through their sons to reach goals that they could never attain.

About four years ago, Drake was leaving a party in East New York, a part of poorest Brooklyn, with a group of friends. Some dudes got out of a car and walked toward the high school basketball star. Two of them were waving guns when the cat with the hoodie yelled for the tall nigga not to move.

Everybody scattered and began running. Both of the thugs started firing wildly at the people. A girl later told the cops that you could hear the string of shots, pop-pop-pop-pop, the bullets whistling in the air past them. Drake stumbled and fell to the pavement and couldn't get up.

When they turned him over, he had two gunshots in the back. One of the parents carried him to his car and sped him to the hospital. Both of the bullets had hit his spinal cord, leaving him crippled from the waist down.

"Damn, they could've shot me in the head and my troubles would have been over," Drake told me when I visited him. "This is totally fucked up."

I completely agreed with him but I would never tell him to his face. God can be sometimes a trickster. Drake had everything in front of him. The good life. Everything. But now he was going to be trapped in that damn chair for life.

"Sure, we're pulling for you and living through you because if you can make the journey to the high life, then we will be a success too," my father said to me while going to the grocery store. "A lot of folks are counting on you. You've got a responsibility to not just yourself but to everybody. Remember that?"

Damn it, I thought. If people let me find my own way, everything would be cool. So much pressure, so much tension. I wanted to blow off steam but I didn't know how. I didn't do anything out of my character, nothing crazy, nothing to make my family ashamed of me.

2 / SHAME THE DEVIL

Joba Duane, a dude who used to play forward on our team, was running around with a crowd of roughnecks; most of them were former jailbirds. After one of the games, Joba offered me a joint but I refused it and man, he called me all kinds of names. So he and the crew were driving around the Bronx one night, and spotted somebody who owed Joba cash money.

"Hey spook, yo' owe me some cash, two large, and you been dodging me for three weeks," Joba shouted at the fleeing dude. "I told you I wants my money. You gon' gimme my money or I'll fuck you up."

The runner, panicked at the threat, fled between parked cars, zigzagging to prevent from getting shot. But the Beemer whipped around, squealed to a stop, and three of Joba's crew opened fire with heavy artillery. Some of the shots raked the front of an apartment building, sending sparks and shattered glass from the rooms with people living in them.

One apartment on the first floor contained a grandfather, an eighty-six-year-old, who was getting up to shut off his TV when the volley of shots came through the window, knocking him flat on the carpet. Later, his wife was on the news at eleven, saying he was reaching for the remote when the shots came through the window. He got it in the right jaw and the center of his chest.

"Henry kept saying I'm shot, I'm shot," his wife, tears in her

eyes, said in a shaky voice to the reporters. "I didn't know what to do. So much blood. I went over to my neighbor's place and we called 9-1-1. Henry is lucky. He could be dead."

The news announcer gave a description of the vehicle, containing four black youths, armed and dangerous. She gave a number to the police tip line, saying all calls would be confidential.

Somebody tipped the cops off. Joba was singled out. The police staked him out for four days before they moved in, tailing him from the loading dock where he worked part-time, and surrounded him in his place. He lived there with his mother, his Dominican girlfriend and her baby. It wasn't his but he took care of it.

"They surrounded the house and moved in, trapping him like a rat," Luz said, clutching her baby. "They kicked down the door, slapped around his mother, and searched for him. He heard them when they came in and he went up the fire escape to the roof. They went up there after him."

"Did you see them shoot him?" the television reporter asked.

"No, they kept us inside," Joba's girlfriend sobbed. "They shot him in his belly, in his neck and in his hand. They said he was wrestling with them for the gun. He didn't have a gun. They shot him down like a dog."

"How is his mother taking it?" the reporter asked.

"What did you think?" Luz snapped. "She collapsed when they brought him out. She heard the sirens and the helicopters...and saw him when they carried him out in a body bag. She's crazy with grief, you know."

Oh man, my Pops, a used-to-be follower of Marcus Garvey and The Honorable Elijah Muhammad, went off about that Joba business. First, he started talking about the crumbling middle class, the recession, and how people were going nuts because the country cannot pay its debts. He babbled about reducing the

deficit and how low-income families weren't ever going to move up the economic ladder.

"That's why these black boys robbin' and stealin' and killin' people, because they can't get any work," Pops added. "Joba didn't have a chance in this country. Most black boys don't have a chance. The cards are stacked against you guys."

I'd listen to him go off about the responsibility of young black men and the need to wake up to what's going on. The men and the boys are letting down the community, letting down the family, letting down the women, letting down the kids. But I couldn't see what he was doing to benefit anybody.

"Dad, somebody called you when you were out, said something about some money owed to a lawyer," I said. "I told him that you would call him back when you got in. He sounded like it was important."

"Everything's fuckin' important," my father growled.

"Are you going to be at the last game?" I asked him. "It's for the championship. The trainer and the coach say I should be ready so I'll play."

My father rubbed his chin and put his hand on my shoulder. "You've got to play your ass off. Coach Faulk said some pro and college scouts are going to be in the stands checking you out. You got to have your A game for that night."

"I will, I will." I grinned.

"Because it's all about the cash, the green stuff." My father lit a cigarette. "This is a capitalist society and everything is about money. You ain't shit until you got some money. Vultures and capitalism go hand in hand. One day I'll explain capitalism to you and how it works. As much money as this country generates, there

should be no unemployment, no foreclosures, no lack, no poverty. The white man has this shit set up where poverty and capitalism go hand in hand. I'll explain it to you one day before you go out in the world."

"Explain what?"

"Explain how the real world operates, son." He took a deep drag of the smoke and let it out through his nostrils. The cigarette habit was something he had picked up recently. He always appeared stressed; jittery; worked up.

Our family had moved out of the projects into a fairly stable neighborhood bordering on a high crime area. For a time, we lived with our aunt in the Pink Houses in the East New York section of Brooklyn, but my father finally got some money coming in and we moved. Still, with all the money coming in the house, my parents were fussing and fighting. Pops accused her of spending money like it was growing on trees. Those were his words.

I plopped down on the couch. "Pops, what do you do? I have no idea what you do for a living. Somebody asked me and I didn't know what to tell them."

He pulled up a chair. It was crazy how much I looked like him. Mini-me. He lit another cigarette, frowned a little and stared out the window.

"What do you do, Pops?" I repeated.

"Hustle." He laughed roughly. "I'm a hustler. Every black man worth his salt is a hustler. If you want to be successful, then you will be a hustler."

I pulled up my feet and stared at him. "Then you're no better than Joba."

"Bullshit. No, Joba was a loser. He accomplished nothing with his life, except to spread misery and suffering. In fact, I'm glad he's dead. You know why I say that?"

"No." I wanted to hear this. Pops was in love with his voice. He loved to hear himself talk.

"Listen to me, son," my father said. "Martin Luther King was a hustler. Adam Clayton Powell was a hustler. Malcolm X was a hustler. Like I said, every black man wanting to do something is a hustler. These black men will do anything to have control in their lives. They want freedom. They want choices. And that is what I want for you. I want you to be a hustler."

At this point, my eyes were glazing over. Yak, yak, yak. I was thinking about going down to the Vicious Juice Bar on Atlantic Avenue, getting one of those frosty fruit smoothies or a Portobello mushroom wrap with sun-dried tomatoes and low-fat Mozzarella cheese. Joyce, my honey, hipped me to this place. She liked this health drink, a shake made with soy milk, protein powder and a little juice. She was on this health kick.

"Are you listening to me, son?" He stood up and got closer.

"Yes...yes." I was still thinking about Yvette. She was probably one of the most beautiful girls in the whole damn world. She was my cover girl and totally out of my league.

"See, that's what wrong with you," Pops said angrily. "And that's what wrong with most black boys and that's why they will not get anywhere in this world."

"That's not going to happen to me," I protested. "I've got potential. That's what everybody says. I'm not like most black boys."

"But hear me out. You must learn how to hustle."

In my mind's eye, I imagined how I would seduce Yvette when I finally got her alone. I almost had her alone on Valentine's Day but one of her lovelies came over to her place. Damn, she was a gorgeous female. Plus Joyce wasn't putting out. She wanted to remain a virgin until we got married. She was dull as shit.

Now, my old man was standing over me, shouting at me like I

was deaf. "If you're soft, you're gonna screw up. I think you're soft. I don't think you have what it takes."

I didn't like him looking down on me.

"Just because you're messed up in your life, Pops, that don't mean I'll do the same," I snapped back at him. "I'll be big one day and you'll see."

I hopped up from the couch and went to the fridge for a glass of Coke. Judging from his expression, I'd rattled his cage and put something on his mind to think about.